Mary Mapes Dodge

Theophilus and Others

Mary Mapes Dodge

Theophilus and Others

ISBN/EAN: 9783743305090

Manufactured in Europe, USA, Canada, Australia, Japa

Cover: Foto ©Andreas Hilbeck / pixelio.de

Manufactured and distributed by brebook publishing software
(www.brebook.com)

Mary Mapes Dodge

Theophilus and Others

THEOPHILUS AND OTHERS.

Theophilus and Others

BY

MARY MAPES DODGE

AUTHOR OF "HANS BRINKER; OR, THE SILVER SKATES,"
"RHYMES AND JINGLES," ETC.

NEW YORK

SCRIBNER, ARMSTRONG, AND COMPANY

1876

TO

L. G. R.

PREFACE.

————◆————

THESE tales and talks, most of which have appeared in various periodicals, are now, at the urgent solicitation of friends, &c., &c., &c.

Their preparation has enlivened hours of, &c., &c., &c.

If this little volume shall, &c., &c.

In conclusion, the author begs, &c., &c., &c.

M. M. D.

CONTENTS.

DOBBS'S HORSE.

IVE years ago, Theophilus and I prepared to realize the dream of our married life. We bought a cottage in the country. This great event really sprang from a tiny speck of ivory that had made more stir in coming into this world than the most enormous tusk ever thrust by elephant into an Indian jungle. I need not add that it was our Philly's first tooth.

Philly, christened Theophilus after his father, stood third on our family record. Being the first male item, he was invested with peculiar interest. Indeed, to our discerning eyes, he at once evinced traits which lifted him far above all other babies in the created world. And now the dear little fellow was teething.

Julie and Nelly had in turn wrestled with a similar experience; but they were only girls. They were not even silent partners in the prospective BROWN & SON, the very thought of which firm had made Theophilus look foolish, and strut about the house, before Philly was a week old. It was only when our parental career entered its third denticurate, that we doubted the force of that modern emendation, —

> "How sharper than a thankless serpent, 'tis
> To have a toothless child!"

What wonder that, as Philly, growing paler and weaker every day, kicked and screamed his protest against the existing order of things, Theophilus became less pompous concerning him; and finally bowed his head meekly at my announcing one mornıng at breakfast, that "something must be done at once." Every truly wedded man knows very well what "something must be done" means when his wife says it. It means penetration. It means compliance. It means that all the hints lately sown on his unsuspecting mind are expected to burst suddenly into full flower. Therefore, when Theophilus heard me say that *something* must be done, he at once responded, —

"Well, my dear, I suppose we shall have to try country air: the child certainly is failing."

The point was gained. My hints had bloomed. But this was only a bud, and I wanted the full-blown flower. So I remarked — with the air of a woman who had other things to think of — that he was right; the baby *was* failing; and, as far as my experience went, I thought that a country hotel or boarding-house would soon finish him.

"Then what is to be done?" cried Theophilus, thoroughly alarmed, and in a highly receptive condition.

Lifting the lid of the coffee-pot, and peering into it with intense interest, I remarked abstractedly, that when people wished to go to the country, and had objections to boarding, they generally hired a cottage or something of that kind.

Now, one need not have gone through Euclid, nor studied Whately, to know that this pretty breakfast scene finally resolved itself into a snug little country-box. To be candid, Theophilus, considering our city expenses, was not in a position to purchase just such a place as we wanted. Our "box" was not all that could be desired: still it was in the country; and imagination festooned its porch with coming vines, and rejoiced in the proposed lawn where our little ones should roll "like tumbled fruit." The advertisement which had attracted us toward the place, described it as being well stocked with trees of every description. In fact, we purchased it mainly on the representations of this same advertisement. Theophilus' had time to pay it only a flying visit after business hours; and, as the owner declared that no less than "six other gentlemen" were eager to pounce upon the prize, we really did not dare to deliberate.

Accordingly, Theoph hired a man-of-all-work, and, before despatching him to the scene of action, gave him a written list of orders, foremost among which were special instructions concerning the aforesaid vines and lawn. There was to be a fine vegetable-patch in the rear; and, as well as I could make out from Theoph's chart, the space between lawn and kitchen-garden was to be filled with roses, honeysuckles, shrubs of all kinds, and showy annuals of every hue imaginable.

"Aren't you afraid, Theoph, dear," I suggested, "you will have rather too much? I like the idea of all this luxuriance; but we must avoid confusion of effect, you know. Beside, it appears to me, you have left scarcely room for us to walk about among the flowers."

"Better to have too much than too little, Emma. It will be very easy to 'thin out' after we are settled, if we find the garden overcrowded. As we have named the place 'Flowery Grove,' it strikes me we can hardly have too many flowers."

"That's true, Theoph: how delightful it will be ! We'll sit out under the vines when you come up from town in the afternoon (so different from that bleak piazza at Stamford); and, while the children are rolling and chasing each other about the lawn, we can read and talk to our hearts' content. Oh, it will be grand ! "

Theoph kissed me, and said in his cheerful way that the very prospect made me look bright and rosy again; but he shook his head gravely when he heard Philly's feeble cry, and asked why in the world we couldn't go there at once. The gardener's wife must have the cottage all cleaned by this time, he said; and I had nothing to do but to go.

With the moths already flying about, it was trying to a woman with five Brussels carpets and all the parlor curtains and furniture on her mind, — to say nothing of the summer's shopping, — to hear the grand business of moving into the country for a summer spoken of so cavalierly; but I conquered the outraged spirit within, and even entered into an amicable consultation with Theophilus concerning the amount of furniture required for our five-room cottage.

His counsel was invaluable. Better to take up almost nothing in the furniture line, he said. We needed only to fit out a comfortable sitting-room, — something a little tasteful, you know ; four or five bedrooms for the family;

a dining-room of some sort; and — oh yes! — a spare room by all means, for he meant to have Dobbs up there half the time; and, above all, plenty of kitchen equipments, for if there was any thing in the world he *did* hate, it was a half-way dinner.

Striving to look as much like St. Cecilia as possible, and yet retain an impressive cast of countenance, I ventured to suggest, at this point, that there were but four rooms in the house besides the kitchen.

"No!" exclaimed Theophilus, staring innocently.

"I have counted them, my dear," I replied, with concentrated quietness of tone.

"You've counted them wrong, then, my love."

"Now, Theoph, do be reasonable. There's the large sitting-room on the first floor: you surely don't call the crockery-closet between it and the kitchen a room?"

"No," said Theophilus meekly, at the same time holding up the first finger of his left hand to represent the sitting-room.

"Then, on the second floor there's the small bedroom for Ellen, over the hall."

Up went another finger.

"Well, the little room makes two; then there's the large front one, where the ceiling was bro " —

"By George!" cried Theoph, dropping his patent tally in a twinkling, "there's Dobbs!"

Alas! Dobbs was indeed crossing the street.

My husband was soon in the hall, holding the front door wide open.

"Hallo! old fellow, how are you?" cried a hearty voice.

2

" All right, thank you.   Walk in, walk in."

Then there was a slight shuffling of boots on the oil-cloth ; and in the next instant I heard the parlor blinds thrust violently open.

" Ha, ha ! " laughed Mr. Dobbs ; "that is something like.   Now one can see out.   Why in the world, Brown, do all you married men keep your parlors so dark ? "

Whatever Theoph's reply may have been, it is to this day locked in the bosom of Mr. Dobbs, for I couldn't hear it.   The question made a deep impression upon me, how-ever ; and after that I took care to have the parlors rather lighter than formerly.

Why Mr. Dobbs should have been so fond of Mr. Brown, and why Mr. Brown so doted on Mr. Dobbs, are questions that I never expect to solve while in the flesh. To spiritual ken the mystery may be revealed clear as day. So I must be patient, and content myself by remarking that, in all the annals of masculine friendship, I have never met with so remarkable a case.

Mr. Dobbs was good enough in his way, but no more like Theoph than I to Hercules.   In the first place, he was one of the restless sort, or, as he forcibly expressed it, " always on the go."   He was a superb gymnast too : Theoph never moved a muscle unnecessarily, and looked forward to a heaven of perfect rest.   Theoph liked style and elegance : Mr. Dobbs despised both.   Mr. Dobbs was soothing and conciliatory : Theophilus was an inveterate tease.   Mr. Dobbs evinced a peculiar distaste for children : Theoph had doted on them since his own toddlehood. Mr. Dobbs was never unconquerable : Theoph's stubborn-ness, when fairly aroused, amounted to inspiration.   Theophilus was extremely fond of music: Mr. Dobbs wished that the heavenly maid had died young. Dobbs delighted to shock one with his moral and social heterodoxy: Theoph was a model of propriety. Theoph was fastidious, too, in his personal habits: Dobbs was careless to a fault. Theoph revelled in the choicest literature: Mr. Dobbs never read a line if he could avoid it.

Yet, I repeat, these two men clung to each other with a love marvellous to behold. The friendship of Damon and Pythias was as nothing compared to it; for the two Syracusans were willing only to die for each other; and these were willing to live in friendship in spite of differences of opinion and taste.

Therefore, when Theophilus discovered that there would be no spare room for his dear Dobbs, he stood transfixed with dismay and a sense of desolation. But Dobbs, nothing discouraged, assured him it was a matter of no consequence at all: he could be stowed away anywhere, — in the barn, under a hen-coop, on the kitchen-dresser, for that matter.

"But," exclaimed my spouse, forgetting proprieties in his despair, "there isn't any dresser, hang it!"

"Well," rejoined Dobbs soothingly, "there'll be a sofa or a table; or we'll swing a hammock somewhere: never fear, man."

Just then Nelly, our bright-eyed little three-year-old, ran into the room.

Mr. Dobbs felt, that, as a friend of the family, he must notice her.

"Come here, sis;" and two fingers beckoned her mechanically.

Nelly drew back. A child can always detect the taint of Herod, cover it as one may.

It was all the same to Mr. Dobbs: he had done his duty. Still, for friendship's sake, he would add one more touch; so he resumed, looking sympathetically first at us, and then at the ruddy little creature, —

"Ah, yes! teething, I think you said. Yes: she looks badly " —

" Ha! ha!" laughed Theophilus. "That's not the baby." Dobbs fell back in a mock swoon. I was too indignant to make any comment. Theophilus, I am sure, would have been disgusted with such stupidity in any other man; but it was only irresistibly funny and fascinating in Dobbs.

The gentleman redeemed himself, however, before the evening was over, by covering the chandeliers for me. Theophilus would as soon have thought of offering to wrap up the moon. I saw him wince, though, when his Damon, taking off his coat, carelessly tossed it on the piano, before proceeding to business.

We were in our country-box at last; and, before we were fairly settled, Philly began to show decided signs of improvement. That was the main thing, of course. But how shall I describe the sense of disappointment with which we gradually awoke to the conviction that our imagination had been far more fertile than our land? that the vines and flowers which had sprung up so profusely there were of exceeding slow growth in actual soil? The "trees of every description" were so young and tender that they were visible only from particular points of view.

Bare was our porch in June; and, but for a neighbor's hint, bare it would have remained. Our gardener's vine was one of the "slow and sure" kind, warranted to cover the lattice in five years; whereas Theoph and I were hardly willing to wait as many days.

The hint proved cheering, however; for, with our neighbor's assistance, we planted morning-glory seed on one side of the porch, and Madeira roots on the other; and, I am happy to say, Theoph and I did sit under the shadow of its vines before the summer was over—that is, when the mosquitoes allowed us the privilege.

As for the velvety lawn, if a wide expanse bearing six stones to each blade of grass constitutes a lawn, we had one with a vengeance. The flower-garden also fell short of our anticipations, certainly as far as luxuriance was concerned. Most of the "showy annuals" were like their modest sisters alluded to by Gray: they "blushed unseen," if they ever blushed at all; for we never saw any thing but their tombstones, or rather the labels which, at the time of planting, Mike had carefully erected over the grave of each particular variety.

The kitchen-garden was more promising; and that was some consolation, after all. For what, as our neighbor Miss Kimso observed, are so delightful as pure, sweet, country vegetables, fresh from "your own vines and fig-trees?" It was a peculiarity of Miss Kimso, be it known, never on any account to use a quotation correctly, though she was overflowing with them at all hours, and upon all occasions. They invariably came either in the wrong place or in the wrong way.

Blithe and agile, apparently nearing her fortieth sum-

2*

mer, with light curls falling, "in a spring-like way," on
either side of a face over which Time had tenderly drawn
his finger, pressing hardest round the mouth and eyes, she
diffused an electric influence that had light rather than
life in it. Her short, quick footfall impressed one with
a sense of the instability of things generally. If there
were strength anywhere, it was in her eye ; but it was the
strength of banded sentiments rather than of thought, —
of kindliness rather than of sacrifice. That a warm heart
was fluttering somewhere in her wisp-like little body, we
soon had ample proof. From the evening of our arrival,
when she ran over with a kettle of hot tea and a dish of
buttered biscuit, saying, by way of apology, that she was a
stranger, but "were we not all men and brothers ?" we
felt that we should like her, whatever might be her peculiarities.

We soon discovered that she lived alone with a colored
servant in her little cottage near by ; but we did not know
for some time of the shadow that in early life had fallen
upon her, and that was now only temporarily lifted.

After a while we began to feel quite comfortable in our
new abode. The servants ceased to complain that the
place was "so dreary-like." As for the children, they were
in Elysium, and revelled and romped from morning till
night. Here and there a flower bloomed on some solitary
spike ; and a faint greenish hue broke out in spots over our
lawn. Our one surviving pear-tree was an unfailing source
of expectant admiration ; and Miss Kimso's cow, with a
tinkling bell swinging from its neck, served to give a rustic
charm to the scene. Besides, the birds exerted themselves
when they found we were not dull-eared country-folk ; and

crickets and katydids gave a pulse to the very air we breathed. Theoph found comfort in the dozens of books which he had smuggled among the baggage, though the children's muddy shoes and their freckled little noses distressed him exceedingly.

The crowning joy of all, however, was our horse and rockaway. Theophilus and I had held many a consultation before we decided upon this piece, or rather these pieces, of extravagance. But there was a snug little barn on the premises, and Philly needed the rides so much, and, in short, we wished it; and when did any one ever cultivate a wish without producing a plentiful crop of good reasons in its favor?

I may inform the trusty reader that our rockaway was second-hand; as good as new, however, or even better, if the representations of Messrs. Jacobs & Co., carriage dealers, could be relied upon. The horse was represented to be a rare combination of physical perfection and all the cardinal virtues. Certainly a prettier, more graceful animal, never trod in harness. His ways, too, were so grand! He would paw the earth with impatient hoof, and curve his neck, as though he felt the blood of old Bucephalus coursing in his veins. The daintiness of his appetite was charming; and for a while our great pastime, whenever he was brought to the door, was to pull up spears of grass for him, and put lumps of sugar, one by one, into his lordly mouth. I used often to lay my cheek against his warm neck, and fancy myself Di Vernon, until one day Mike startled me with, —

"Have a care, or he'll be steppin' on yer foot, mum! He was near takin' the toes off meself this mornin'."

I sprang back, knocking Julie and Nelly over in the act.

"Why, Mike, you don't mean to say that there's any thing vicious about him, do you?"

"Well, indade, mum, perraps he's not afther knowin' that your fate's any tinderer thin his own is," he answered, adjusting the harness as he spoke ; "and the flies has him oneasy like. Would ye be wantin' me to drive, mum, or is the gentleman intendin' to go?"

"I shall drive," answered Theophilus, stepping from the porch.

When we were all in, — two on the front seat, and two on the back, — Mike retreated a few steps, and, without raising his eyes, said, —

"Would ye be stoppin' at the village, sir?"

"Yes," replied Theoph, tightening the reins. "Why?"

"There's hay a-wantin,' sir, if ye'd plaze spake till them about it down to the bridge."

Theoph nodded, and off we started. The horse went beautifully, and his driver was in high spirits.

"There's a stride for you!" he exclaimed, after a moment's silence. "Free as air ; isn't it?"

If Theophilus has one weakness greater than another, it is for fine horses.

After we had stopped at the village post-office, attended to a little marketing, and left an order for the hay, Theoph turned the horse's head homeward.

"I say, Em, this is a glorious animal! I can sell him in the fall for double his cost. Why in the world Jacobs let me have him for a hundred and fifty, I cannot conceive."

"He belonged to Jacobs's brother, you remember, who was going unexpectedly to California," I said.

"Yes," returned Theoph; "but Jacobs was probably ignorant of his worth. He said he knew nothing at all about horse-flesh. He's descended from the famous Black Prince, you know."

"Who? Jacobs?" I asked, in astonishment.

"No: the horse. It strikes me, Emma," continued Theophilus between his teeth, "you're inclined to be rather facetious this morning."

"Oh, not at all, darling! go on. I love to hear you talk about the beautiful creature."

"Who? Jacobs?"

Of course I pouted now. Theoph would have been quite restored to good humor by his own joke, had not the horse's tail become heavily entangled in the lines at this moment.

"That rascally Mike has forgotten the fly-net again! The fellow is too careless for any thing!"

"It *is* provoking," I assented amiably; "especially as I called to him, while he was harnessing the horse, not to forget it."

"By the way, Em," said Theophilus, freeing the lines with a skilful flourish, "I heard you calling from the window, 'Mi-eke, Mi-eke!' and do you know, dear, it jarred me. If the man had any other name, I should not mind it; but 'Mike' is so horribly plebeian! Mike here, Mike there: it really sounds badly, indeed it does, and has an unhappy effect upon the children. This nicknaming of servants is terrible."

"Very well," said I meekly: "we can call him 'Michael,' if you prefer it." 2

"That is not much better," persisted Theoph. "Call him by his surname: that's the only way, — O'Brian, or Riley, or whatever it may be. Everybody does so nowadays."

So when we drove up to the front-door, and our master of horse duly presented himself, Theoph accosted him abruptly with, —

"Here, fellow, what is your last name?"

"Me last name, sir," stammered the man in great astonishment, "I never had but the one, sir."

"Well, what is it?"

"It's Mike, it is, yer honor."

"Mike *what?*" roared Theophilus.

"Och! I ax yer pardon, sir, — Mike Deerey. It's yerself writ it in yer buk the day I was afther comin' to ye, sir."

"It will sound beautifully, Theoph, won't it?" said I wickedly, as we entered the cottage together. "I can say, 'Bring the horse to the door at five, Deerey.' 'Don't forget the fly-net, Deerey.' Nothing could be more aristocratic."

Theoph tried to laugh good-naturedly; but I know it was something besides our Deerey's carelessness that caused him to be discharged about a week afterward.

One bright morning in June, it occurred to me that there could not be the slightest possible harm in taking the nurse and children to the village myself. The rockaway was in perfect order; and Prince was so gentle, that, as Jacobs had said, a baby could manage him. Besides, Miss Kimso would be delighted to accompany me: she declared that she wasn't at all afraid of horses, and would gladly "hold the noble Rosinante" while I was in the store.

Accordingly our party was soon ready to start. Miss Kimso and I were on the front seat; and Ellen the nurse, Philly, and the two little girls, were compactly stowed away in the rear.

It was a lovely day; and we enjoyed our ride to the utmost. Philly actually crowed with delight; and his sisters, when they ceased complaining that they were "so cwowded," laughed and sang with glee.

A pleasant letter from my dear friend Mary C—— was handed me at the village post-office; our purchases were made, and we were turning out of the village; when suddenly an unusual sound in that region broke upon us, — the sound of a brass band in the distance, playing that inspiriting air, "The Campbells are coming." It proceeded from a showy-looking wagon that was moving slowly toward us. The effect was really charming. Nelly cried, "So-jers, so-jers!" and but for the nurse would have sprung from the rockaway in her excitement. I chirruped to Prince, and gave myself up to the pleasure of the moment.

The notes grew more distinct. Flags were waved merrily from the approaching wagon, and Master Prince stood stock-still, and pricked up his ears.

"Ah!" said Miss Kimso, rolling up her eyes, "'Music hath charms to soothe the savage beast:' let him listen."

Prince *did* listen; and, listening, he concluded to accompany the music with a merry dance. He pranced, he ambled, he chasséed; and finally he stood on his hind legs, and bowed to an imaginary partner before commencing the grand galopade.

Ellen and the children screamed, Miss Kimso with a shriek clutched at the reins, and I instantly recalled every cross word I had ever said to Theophilus.

In a moment two men had the descendant of the Black Prince by the head, and were speaking soothingly to him.

"Whoa, boy! whoa, boy!"

His royal highness, after a few more flourishes and fantastic turns, subsided into a pathetic tremble.

"Jim," said one of the men in a low tone, "there's one of them blasted circuses a-comin': you'd best drive the ladies home. It's Miss Brown, you know,—the Yorkers that bought Weeks's cottage. Couldn't that young woman there on the back seat walk home?" he continued, looking toward Ellen, and raising his voice. "It ain't more'n a mile an' a 'alf."

"It's *two*," muttered the other man: "it's a good two."

Ellen was glad enough to get out.

"An' will I carry the child, mum?" she asked, composing her skirts with one hand while supporting Philly, professionally, with the other.

"Oh no, he's too heavy!" cried Miss Kimso, jumping nimbly over to the back seat. "Here, hand him to me, the sweet, budding innocent. I'll take good care of him."

Jim sprang in beside me, and drove off cautiously amidst a shower of "Thank yous" from Miss Kimso and myself.

Just before we came to a bend in the road, Master Prince began to prick up his ears again. Jim gave me the reins in a twinkling. "Good land!" he exclaimed, jumping out, and seizing the animal by the head, "he smells somethin' a-comin', depend on it!"

Indeed he did,—two great elephants, and a party of horsemen. We could see them distinctly now.

"Keep yer seats, ladies: there ain't no danger!" panted Jim, as the horse's head gave his arm some pretty vigorous jerks. "There, whoa, boy! whoa, whoa!"

Strange to say, Prince faced the elephant more bravely than he did the music. He twitched and trembled all over at first, and seemed ready to drop with fear; but the man's voice and touch gradually re-assured him.

It was an old elephant and her young one. What wonder that a poor little horse should quiver and start beside that mighty bulk and ponderous tread?

The young elephant stalked closely beside its mother, and by the senseless flourishes of its trunk, and the twitches of its stumpy little tail, betrayed a youthful spirit that time and worldly cares had quite subdued in the parent.

"O mamma!" cried Julie, as soon as her astonishment would allow her to speak, — "O mamma, *do* look! see the dear little baby elephant! Isn't he too cunnin'?"

"Yes, dear, very," I responded abstractedly, looking anxiously at Prince, who was about one-third of the dear little creature's size.

We reached home without any further mishap. Theophilus and Mr. Dobbs who had come up by an early train, stood by the gate to welcome us.

Theoph gave one of his queer looks, as he spied the coatless youth beside me; but Dobbs took in the thing at a glance:

"Aha! Horse has been a little fractious, hey?"

Then you should have heard Theoph!

Text: Woman's driving.

The next day, after dinner, my husband blandly proposed a drive. "Will you go, Em?" said he.

"Not to-day, dear, thank you. I have lost my confidence in Prince somewhat."

2*

"Nonsense, Em! I'd like to see the horse I can't manage. Besides, one doesn't meet elephants in this latitude every day. Put on your things, love : we'll drive to Llewellyn Park."

Llewellyn Park was always a conquering temptation with me. While putting on my bonnet, I saw our new man Kelly drive Prince to the door. The beautiful creature looked so gentle, and pawed the ground so reflectively, that my foolish fears were gone in an instant. I called out of the window to my spouse, —

"Shall we take Philly, dear ? "

"Certainly, by all means," he replied, "if the little dumpling is not too heavy for you."

"I'll hold her," called up Mr. Dobbs, looking utterly wretched in an instant.

"Oh, no!" laughed Theoph. "Let the nurse come also, Em. There is plenty of room." Then I heard him say in a severe undertone to his friend, —

"How often must I tell you, Dobbs, that the baby is a boy? — Theophilus Brown, junior: now don't forget it again."

" Beg his pardon, really; but you see the name 'Philly' misled me. I thought it was Phillis. The rest of the children are all girls ; ain't they, Brown? " he asked, in a tone of deep interest.

We were off at last. Prince, thoroughly penitent, never went better. If any thing, he showed scarcely enough spirit: still he was superb, and Theoph and I were very proud of him, especially as people in the neighborhood began by this time to know who we were.

"He's a free goer," said Mr. Dobbs, regarding him

critically. "Hallo! he doesn't interfere a little in the hind legs, does he?"

"Of course not," rejoined Theoph scornfully. "Why, look at him, man! There's not a sounder set of legs anywhere. Did you notice his breadth of chest?"

"No; but I see he's uncommon high in the flanks. He'd make a racer, Brown, that horse would!"

Theoph grew radiant.

"Give him the reins, Brown. George! what a neck he has! He's kind, too, depend upon it. Not one animal in a hundred but would have run like all creation, coming suddenly upon an elephant in that way."

"Certainly," assented Theoph, growing ecstatic: "I don't want any better test than that. You could walk him up to a whole menagerie, sir!"

Just then we heard a shout, and a muddy white pig came dashing through a farm-gate.

I have a vague remembrance of clutching wildly for the baby, of seeing Dobbs high up in the air, of my cheek being dragged against the gravel, and of scrambling to my feet just in time to see Prince dashing off madly in the distance with our rockaway, minus top and passengers.

What bundle was that lying heavily on the bushes beside the road? Theoph was picking it up. It was Philly. Paralyzed at the sight, I managed to gasp out, "O Theoph! is he dead?"

"No, all right!" he shouted, clasping the terrified little creature to his heart. "There's not a scratch on him, thanks to those good bushes!"

"Hallo, Brown!" exclaimed a dusty figure sitting in the middle of the road; "allow an old sinner to correct you. I'd give a little credit to Providence, if I were you."

"Dobbs, my dear fellow, you all safe too? Yes, indeed, we have reason to thank Providence!" he exclaimed fervently.

"For which, the escape or the accident?" asked the incorrigible Dobbs, getting up slowly, and knocking the dust from his clothes.

"For both," returned Theoph solemnly. "Good gracious, Emma, look at your cheek!"

I couldn't very well look at my cheek, under the circumstances; and, as I certainly-felt no sensation there, I scarcely noticed his exclamation, but ran over to Ellen, the nurse, who sat upon the grass looking wildly about her.

Theophilus and Mr. Dobbs stood her upon her feet, and worked her arms like pump-handles. There were certainly no bones broken. Yet she seemed bewildered, and unable to walk.

"O Theoph dear! she is injured internally," I cried in distress. "One of you must run to Orange for a doctor."

"Howly Fathers! where am I?" broke forth the poor girl at last.

"You're all safe now, Ellen," I replied, kneeling beside her, and putting my arm tenderly round her shoulder. "We have been thrown from the carriage. See, here's dear little Philly: don't you know him?"

Theoph held the baby on her lap. In an instant she caught him in her arms, and kissed him over and over again, sobbing as if her heart would break.

"Och, me darlin', me darlin'! Is it kilt ye are? Ah, my poorty baby! Bad luk to the murtherin' baste, thin!"

We knew she was all right now. This point settled, I suddenly felt a great tingling in my left cheek. Mr.

Dobbs and Theoph were talking together, I heard the latter say hurriedly, —

"Yes: you may try. Somebody has probably caught him before this. I must stay, and attend to Em."

By this time, there were several persons around us, — two teamsters, a sprinkling of deeply entertained children, and one fleshy lady, bearing a pitcher of water and a bundle of rags, who declared it was "the most mirac'lous accident" she ever heard of.

The men were soon busily examining the remnants of our rockaway-top, lifting broken bits of iron, wood, and any amount of leather and torn-cushion arrangements.

"If it hadn't a-bin sich a rotten old thing, it would a-gone harder with you," observed one of the men sententiously to my crestfallen Theophilus.

"Yes: it must have went all to pieces at the first go," remarked the other teamster reflectively.

The fat lady conducted our dilapidated party to her cottage near by, and in true Oriental style gave us water, and bade us wash, and be welcome. My cheek proved to be badly scraped; but Theophilus, bless his heart! is the tenderest nurse in the world, and soon made me comparatively comfortable.

Our habiliments, though, were past repair. Such looking objects as we were! My "love of a bonnet" was a hopeless wreck. As for Theoph's clean linen "duster," it was past redemption by either soap or needle. Ellen was all excitement, and remembered the accident in its minutest particulars.

"Och! indade, ma'am," she repeated again and again, "but it was oreful. I saw the horris give one lep; and

8*

thin over we wint all forninst the other! but I never once-t
let go the dear child, ma'am, but jist held on till him
through it all.   If ye'll belave me, ma'am, I gathered his
very cloak around him: so I did."

After setting our hearts all aglow with the thought that
God's children were good and kind to each other after all,
our adipose friend sent us home in her only vehicle, — a
farm-wagon filled with clean straw.

To our astonishment, as we neared the house, we saw
Mr. Dobbs and the man rubbing down Prince, who, steam-
ing and panting, stood near a cart-like looking affair that
proved on inspection to be the remains of our lovely,
"better-ash-new" rockaway.   He had dashed in with it at
a furious rate, much to the consternation of our home
force.

Poor Miss Kimso, standing in her doorway, declared
that she had been struck motionless with terror. "I tried,"
she said, "to ask my Phœbe to run over and find out what
had happened; but the words 'stuck in my throat' — like
Macbeth's dagger.   Oh, what a mercy it is that you're all
safe!"

A lame, aching party were we the next day.   Mr. Dobbs
was sorely bruised, and couldn't think of going to town.
Theoph and Kelly took Prince back to Mr. Jacobs, and
entered their complaint.

All the satisfaction they could get was that "he vash
not a horsh-dealer — it vash his brudder's horsh — he know
notting 'bout him — his brudder vash gone to Canadah" —

"You told me California," interrupted poor Theoph.

"Vell, vat if I did?" retorted Mr. Jacobs, in no way
disconcerted.   "My brudder vill go to both country 'fore

he come home. You ax me take de horsh off you hand? Vat for? I no vant him. A horsh run vay vonce, he ish no vorth zat " (snapping his fingers).

Just as Theoph, after a despairing protest, was about to leave the spot in disgust, accompanied by Kelly and the Prince, Jacobs called him back.

" I tell you vat I vill do ; and I can do no more. I cannot give you pig price for runavay horsh ; he ish not vort tventy dollar. But I vill do zis. You say you carriage all broke ; vell, I vill give you good coupé, most so good ash new, for him : vat you say to zat, hey ? "

At first the offer was rejected with disdain ; but finally my Antonio, not having his Portia there to attend to the case, let it go by default. The (horse) flesh fell to Shylock, and the coupé was sent to " Flowery Grove " by the evening train.

The only excuse Theophilus gave on his return to that prematurely named spot, was that he could not conscientiously sell the animal to any one else ; and he knew carriage number one was past repairing. As to another horse, he really did not know how in the world he could spare the money to get one just then ; but he would try to manage it somehow.

At this point Damon came to the rescue of his Pythias.

" Brown," he exclaimed, springing from a recumbent position, and slapping Theophilus on the shoulder, " have I been asleep? Why in the world didn't I think of it before ? There's just the very animal you want, over in Westchester County, waiting for you to come and take him."

Theoph stared hopefully, and Mr. Dobbs continued,

"Just the very thing, I tell you. A good, sound family horse ; not young, but all the safer for that. Has been a splendid-looking creature in his day ; but the people up there have let him go down a little. All they care for is to get the price of his board. I have had my misgivings of late, that it's not exactly the right place for him. All you need do is to have him brought here at once. You will soon get him in high condition, and may have the full use of him for his keep. There you are, my man ! Hold ! I'll *give* him to you, though there's not another man in the world that should have him."

Pythias thanked him heartily, and declared that he thought, under the circumstances, it would be about the best thing for both sides.

"Certainly it would, my boy ; certainly it would," said Damon, tumbling back again on the sofa. "We'll have him here at once."

As an interested spectator to the scene, I could not help wondering why Mr. Dobbs, who evidently was not burdened with a surplus of worldly treasure, should have assumed the expense of keeping a horse in this way. Theophilus relieved me by asking the question point-blank.

Mr. Dobbs replied rather gruffly, —

"He belonged to my mother," and closed his eyes with pretended drowsiness. I saw his lip tremble though, and from that hour have loved him in spite of his queer notions.

The horse was on a farm in Westchester County, near the old cottage where our friend had lived through his happy childhood, and where his parents had, within a year of each other, ended their days. A simple marble slab in the village churchyard, bearing the inscription " Father and Mother," marks their resting-place. An old woman, living near the spot, has told me that she saw a tall, dark-haired gentleman planting the ivy and roses there with his own hands.

Great was my surprise, on the second day after our upsetting, to receive a note from Theophilus, saying that he would not be up that night, and that he wished Mr. Dobbs, "lame or not, to come down, without fail, by the first train. No cause for alarm," the letter added ; it was "only a business affair requiring immediate attention," &c.

On the next evening Theoph came back alone.

"Well, Em," he exclaimed, while kissing all three of the children at once, " Dobbs is off ! "

" Off ! Where ? "

"Why, he's gone. Gone to California. A splendid opening for him turned up yesterday. He saw the parties last night, and was off this afternoon at a few hours' notice. The energy of that man is prodigious ! "

" How long will he be away ? "

" Oh ! perhaps three months, perhaps a year ; can't tell. Where's Kelly ? Down in the village ? "

" Yes. Why ? "

" I shall have to send him to Westchester by the first train to-morrow morning. Dobbs's horse is to be brought down."

" That is good news ! " I exclaimed, quite delighted. " But how did you have an opportunity to make the arrangements ? "

3

"Oh! Dobbs thinks of every thing. You never saw any thing like it. Just before he started, he handed me this letter, which he says will make it all right with Fowler, the man who has the horse. The last thing he said, as the boat was let go, was, 'Take care of old Charley, my boy. "Love me, love my dog," you remember.' And then he waved his handkerchief, and was off."

It was strange to hear Theoph sigh. But we took a walk around the place together; found an isolated flower or two; counted, for the twentieth time, the four pears on our tree; watched the chickens; looked into the stable to see that all was comfortable there for the expected steed; congratulated each other upon the treasure we should have in "Charley;" and by tea-time Theoph was quite cheerful.

All the next day our household, Philly excepted, was in a fever of expectation; and when six o'clock came (the time when Kelly and the horse were expected to make their appearance), the excitement was intense. Even Miss Kimso ran over to witness, as she said, the arrival of

"The gallant young man on a spirited steed."

The two little girls clapped their hands, and played about the lawn, in joyful anticipation; and the cook, housemaid, and Ellen were constantly running in turn to the front gate, screaming, "There he comes! No, it's a wagon, sure." "Faith, he's bringing *two* horses, mum. Oh, no, it's the stage that's comin'!" At last Ellen cried out in a tone of unmistakable certainty, —

"An' by the powers, mum, here he is! Well, if iver I saw the like!"

Heralded by this announcement, Kelly (yclept "Pat" by his intimates) rode in state through the grand entrance, now officiously thrown open by Julie and the cook. Theophilus, who had been trying to read Motley with dignified composure in the meagre shade of the pear-tree, threw down his book, and came forward.

There we all stood, an eager group, every eye intent upon Charles and his rider. Kelly appreciated his opportunity, and tried for once "to witch the world with noble horsemanship." Alas! it was useless. Feeling that an apology was required, he exclaimed, after jerking angrily at the bridle without producing any visible effect, —

"Ah, sir, divil a bit off uv a walk would he move for me the day! The crayture's bones is a'most through the skin, sir."

At the peroration of this startling address, he presented a side-view to the assembled spectators. The effect was electric. Theophilus looked tragic, Miss Kimso almost fainted, Ellen and Kitty giggled, and the cook clapped her hands on her knees, and laughed immoderately.

"Faith, he's a jewel, sir," said Kelly, with a grin, sliding down from the animal's back, and gaining courage from the sounds around him. "Upon me sowl, sir, I'm thinkin' it's feedin' him on barrels they've bin, if seein' the staves betokens any thing."

"Silence!" commanded Theophilus.

"Will I take him yonder to the stable, sir?" asked Kelly, sobered in an instant.

"Yes. Stay!" said Theophilus, with some hesitation. "Are you sure you've made no mistake, that you've brought the right horse?"

"Faith, sir," answered Kelly, brightening, "it's meself axed that same, sir. But there wasn't, barrin' this one, another horris in it. Perraps the lether, sir, will tell yez about it," he continued, as, after tugging at his pocket for a minute or so, he succeeded in producing a crumpled note.

"Yes, it's all right," said Theoph, after reading the missive, and handing it to me with a hopeless air.

"Theoph, dear," I ventured soothingly, as soon as we were alone, "we may as well take it as a joke. It's the funniest thing that has ever happened to us : so why not laugh at it?"

"Humph!" replied my spouse stiffly. "If you can see any fun in our keeping that snuff-colored skeleton for the rest of his days, you're very welcome. What in the world Dobbs was thinking of in saddling me with that lank, long-backed, high-hipped affair, I cannot conceive."

"But he had not seen him for some time," I urged, knowing that the best way to get Theoph into a good humor was to take his Damon's part. "He told us the horse would probably be in bad condition, you know."

"Yes, so he did. Let Dobbs alone for being fair and honest. Well, care and good feeding possibly may bring up the old nag, after all. He said he *had* been a splendid animal, didn't he?"

"Certainly he did. Everybody knows what a difference a little flesh makes with a horse. When once we get him fattened up and well brushed, and all that sort of thing, he will be a different creature ; and, after all, it's a great comfort to know that he will be perfectly safe and trusty."

"Now, Em," said Theoph appealingly, and working

himself into a heat as he proceeded, "why *do* you say that? A poor horse is never trusty. I've told you so a dozen times! I tell you, Em, I'd rather " —

" O Papa ! " cried Julie, rushing into the sitting-room in great excitement, " our new horse's got 'most no tail at all, Kelly says, only 'bout a dozen hairs, and " —

" Yes, yes, my dear, never mind what Kelly said ; go and wash your face, and don't scream so about the house."

" But, Papa ! " —

" Well ? "

" One of the new horse's eyes opens just as wide as any thing, and the other's 'most shut. Isn't that the Blind Staggers ? "

"There's a skeleton in every house," says some old croaker, I forget who ; and sometimes one can't help believing that it is so. *Our* skeleton most emphatically was old Charley. Rubbing, brushing, combing, blanketing, feeding the creature, were of no avail : a skeleton he remained. To be sure, when compelled to use him, we managed to conceal his anatomy by means of an elaborate fly-net, adding a sort of double nightcap arrangement which went over his ears, and, with its dangling tassels, gave a slightly animated effect. This arranged, Kelly, by tightening the check-rein so as to raise the long neck to a slight angle with the back, and plying the whip industriously, strove to keep up appearances while conveying us to church or to the village. My lazy Theophilus was forced to walk to and from the station every day, for he couldn't and wouldn't drive the creature ; but Miss Kimso and myself sometimes, on rare occasions, assumed that

3*

responsibility.   That this was a mortification both to the flesh and to the spirit, I will not deny.   But the baby needed mountain air; and Kelly, who was coachman, foot-man, stable-boy, gardener, and wood-cutter, all in one, could not always make it convenient to accompany us.

Numerous were the trials that assailed us on these occa-sions.   Dear blundering Miss Kimso often wished that in some magic way we could substitute for him the famous winged horse Parnassus, or that, "like the pauper in the poem, he would at least —

'Rattle his bones over the stones.'"

Not he.   In fact, the only moments in which the idea of motion could be associated with old Charley were those when, by suddenly standing stock-still in the middle of the road, he sent a dazed consciousness through you that he must have been moving an instant before.

One beautiful breezy day, after purchasing supplies at the village store, Miss Kimso and I sprang gayly into our seats, sure of a pleasant drive homeward.

"Come, Charley," said I, in my cheeriest, friendliest tone, as I caught up the reins.

He evidently misunderstood me; perhaps I should have said, "Go, Charley."   But it was too late now.   He did not stir.

For a full half-hour we coaxed, commanded, wheedled, and exhorted that animal, in vain.

Meantime ragged boys and idle men gathered about us.

"Give him some pepper!" shouted one.   "Build a fire under him!" screamed another; and one and all, poking and pushing, shouted, "*Get* up!" and "Now for it!" until

we were ready to cry from mortification. At last, by dint
of hard pulling and urging, with three fresh men at his
head and four stout fellows standing like pall-bearers at
the wheels, we attained that soul of the universe, motion.
After one ecstatic moment of speed, we crawled off, followed by the cheers of the crowd.

In simple justice, however, to the venerable Charles, it
must be stated, that balking was not a frequent practice
with him. As a general rule, he jogged along at a regular gait, engrossed in brown study ; and it was only when,
apparently, the subject under consideration became too
much for him, that he stopped short, in order to take it
up deliberately in all its possible bearings. I really did
not dare to tell Theophilus of this little peculiarity, lest
my career as a whip should suddenly be ended by imperial command. With his high sense of honor, and the
claims of friendship, I knew he would keep old Charley
at any cost; and the luxury of another horse was not to
be thought of for an instant. Poor Theoph felt the de-
privation keenly ; but he never hesitated when following,
as he believed, the simple line of duty. He would be true
to Dobbs, and Dobbs's horse, whatever might happen.
Sometimes, from his high altitude, he would try to regard
Charley as a real treasure, or, as his friend Sparrowgrass
would say, "a most excellent thing to have in the country ;" but this was carrying high-toned principle a little
too far.

One afternoon my husband came from town by an
earlier train than usual. I should have been alarmed,
had I not heard him whistling "*Il Segreto*" as he walked
up the path.

"Em!" he shouted, bustling into the cottage, "want to go to town to-night? I've taken seats at the Academy. They're going to have 'Lucrezia Borgia' for the last time this season."

"O Theoph!" I cried in dismay. "How could you? You know I cannot possibly leave the children."

"Yes, you can, my dear. I have made arrangements for Aunt Ann to come up by the half-past five train on purpose."

"Oh, thank you, Theoph! What a dear, thoughtful creature you are! But"— And my heart sank at a thought which flashed upon me.

"But what?" asked Theoph impatiently.

"My bonnet!" I faltered. "I have no bonnet."

"No bonnet! Why, what in the world did you wear to the village yesterday?"

"Oh! that was a distressed old thing. My best one was ruined on that day" —

"*What* day?"

"Why, the day when Prince ran away with us. Don't you remember?"

Theoph did remember perfectly, of course; but he wished to go to the opera, and so would not admit any thing in reference to the damaged head-gear. He flung the tickets upon the sitting-room table, and asked, with an injured air, what was to be done?

Suddenly his mood brightened. "I have it! Wear one of those worsted things — what do you call them? Riggle — riggle — something."

"Rigolette!" I laughed. "Yes: so I can. My rigolette will answer admirably; but — oh, dear — how can I wear it coming home to-morrow? No lady would wear such a thing, travelling in the daytime."

Theoph threw up his arms in desperation.

"Well, if it's not easier to start a ship-of-war than a woman any time! There are hats in New York, I presume. You can buy one in the morning."

Prudence forbade the suggestion that ladies were also not in the habit of shopping by daylight in rigolettes. Trusting that somebody at Aunt Ann's would lend me a bonnet for the purpose, I hastened from the room, in fine spirits, to make the necessary arrangements for our departure.

In an instant Theoph called out, in a tone of despair, —

"Em, it's no use! The next train doesn't stop at this station, and there is no other until nine o'clock."

"Never mind," I called back, leaning over the baluster. "The 5.30 train stops at Orange."

"But Orange is six miles off," groaned Theoph.

"What if it is?" I responded cheerily. "Old Charley can take us if we start in time."

"Hurrah! so he can; and stop for Aunt Ann too at our depot on his return. Hurry, dear."

Our turnout didn't look so very badly, after all, when Kelly, arrayed in his best clothes, drove around to the door. That fly-net was certainly a great institution. After kissing the children a dozen times, and thanking Miss Kimso for her kind offer to remain with them until Aunt Ann's arrival, we sprang into the coupé, and directed Kelly to drive with all practicable speed to the Orange Depot.

Charley seemed determined to do his best; and Theoph, leaning back complacently, remarked, "If we keep on at this rate, we shall have time enough and to spare."

Before we had proceeded half a mile, however, my unfortunate spouse suddenly clapped his hands on his pockets, looked blank, and gasped, —

"There! I have left the tickets in the pocket of my other coat. Stop, Kelly; we must go back for them: there's ample time."

Kelly turned toward home; and Charley, well pleased at the change, started off at quite a lively pace. More for the sake of saying something than for any other reason, I remarked that I thought I saw him throw them on the sitting-room table. Quick as a wink Theoph clapped his hands on his pockets again.

"No — all right — I have them. I remember now picking them up the last thing. — Turn around again, Kelly."

Order easily given, and, one would suppose, easily obeyed. But, alas! what can willing mind avail against obstinate matter? Kelly pulled the rein, "get up'd," shouted, and plied his whip — all to no purpose. He even stood up to give additional vigor to his strokes; then jumped out, and took "the baste" insinuatingly by the head. Charley's determination was evident. Go forward he would: turn around again he would not.

"Then, by the powers!" exclaimed Kelly, seating himself with new energy, and lashing his horse forward, "but I'll get ahead of ye yet, yer varmint!"

"What are you going to do now?" cried Theoph.

"I'm going up a bit, sir, to the next turn there by the churrich. If I can just kape his attintion till we get onto the other road, it's all right wid yez yet."

Theoph looked admiringly at Kelly, and whispered something to me about "native wit;" but I was too much discouraged to listen.

The ruse succeeded. Charley turned down the next road during one of his fits of brown study, and was soon going once more, slowly but surely, toward the station.

After proceeding a few miles farther, we saw our train, far in the distance, hissing its way along like some great reptile.

"All right!" exclaimed Theoph. "We'll catch it yet, if this old bag of bones doesn't tumble down."

Now, what decent, high-minded horse could be expected to stand such a remark as this?

Charles stopped short.

"Get up!" shouted Kelly, in a tone of alarm.

The distant train became more distinct.

"Get up, you baste!"

We could almost count the cars.

"Ge-et up!"

The smoke-pipe would soon be visible.

"Arrah! be gar! *whill* ye get up?"

Charles stood after the manner of a kitchen-bench, — legs all out at an angle of forty-five.

"I'll tell ye what, sir," said Kelly, laying down the lines, "there's nothin' for yez but ter get out an' walk. It's not near a quarter-mile, sir, and ye'd be there in time. They wait a good bit takin' in water."

Springing out with alacrity, — for I was not going to miss the opera after all this trouble, — I led the way resolutely, and Theoph followed.

"This is what I call seeking pleasure under difficulties," he panted, gaining my side as I hurried on.

"Yes, but it's worth it," said I: "we can rest in the cars."

And so we might have rested in the cars, had not the locomotive, with a fiendish shriek, dashed out of the depot with the whole train, just as we were within twenty feet of the platform.

Shall I enter into the details of that exciting six-mile walk homeward, or tell how we hastened in the hope that we still might find Charley *in statu quo ;* how we had the agony of seeing him, in the distance, finally yield to Kelly's labors ; how Theophilus called and shouted in vain, as the equipage rattled homeward hopelessly in advance of us ; how we still flew on, and trusted that Charley, who never ran so before nor since, would take a rest, and enable Kelly to hear our beseeching cry ; how, finally, we did over-take them just before we reached our own gate ; and how Aunt Ann came puffing up to the door quite indignant that no carriage had been sent to the station to meet her? No.   Rather let the reader fancy us sleeping sweetly and calmly that night after our unwonted exercise.

Let him also imagine my emotions when, in the dead of night, I was wakened by a mysterious thumping, appar-ently within three inches of my head.

I sprang to the floor.   The window was open ; but it was too dark to see any thing.   Presently the thump-ing was repeated, and I heard Kelly's voice outside call-ing, —

"Are ye there, sir ? "

" What is the matter ? " I asked, terror-stricken.

" It's himself I'm wantin', mum.   The horris is very bad.   Would ye ask him to come till the stable, mum ? "

" Theoph, Theoph ! " I cried, " wake up.   Old Charley's sick."

He gave a dismal moan at the name, but never stirred.

"Theoph [shaking him vigorously], Theophilus! old Charley's sick, — dying, perhaps : oh, *do* wake up! What would Mr. Dobbs say, if " —

"Dobbs be hanged!" muttered Theoph, glaring wildly at me. "There goes the train!" and he tumbled back on his pillow like a forty-pounder.

After rummaging frantically for the matches, I lit a candle. By this time Philly was awake, and screaming lustily. Theoph yielded to our combined efforts.

"What *is* the matter?" he asked, sitting up and rubbing his eyes. "Is the baby sick?"

"No. Kelly wants you to go to the stable. I'm afraid old Charley's dying."

"You don't say so!" exclaimed Theoph, leaping up with great alacrity. "If he is very bad, we'll probably want whiskey, or something of that kind, Em, and hot water ; perhaps four pails too, so that we can soak all of his feet at once," he added, chuckling. In fact, I never saw Theoph in better spirits, though he seemed resolved to do all he could to save the poor beast.

Soon after Theoph went out, Kelly came to ask for the "dimmyjohn, mum."

"Och! but there's a hape in it!" he exclaimed, shaking it as he walked out.

Next, Theoph ran into the house for a long-necked bottle, with which to administer the whiskey. We had quite a long search before we found one, especially as the wind blew out our candle three times. At last we were successful. I put on a big shawl over my wrapper, and went with Theoph to hold the lantern.

4

We found Kelly in excellent spirits, and more talkative than was his wont amidst

" The din and telltale glare of noon."

Poor Charley took the whiskey quietly enough, though he had a kind of spasm afterward. His struggles were really frightful.

" Rub his legs, Kelly," said Theoph.

" Ah, begorra, sir," answered Kelly, obeying after a fashion, " I wouldn't be after throubbling meself about the crayture, sir. It's dyin' he is, anyhow. Arrah ! an' it'll be an aise till his bones to be under the sod. Divil a wooden overcoat he'll be wantin', at all ! "

Soon wearying of this style of eloquence, I put the lantern upon the ground, and returned alone to the house. Theoph followed in a few moments.

" Em," he called, " where can I find some wood ? I shall have to make a fire, and heat some water. Can't you wake Bridget or Kitty ? "

Rather than call up the poor girls, who had gone to bed " worn out with their week's ironing," I assisted my comfort-loving spouse through this mighty performance, and smiled to hear him whistling " *Il Segreto* " as he thrust in stick after stick.

" How is Charley now ? " I asked, as soon as the blaze was fairly started.

" Pretty bad ; may get over it, though. We've given him a stiff dose of whiskey ; and I told Kelly to rub his legs (the *horse's* legs, Mrs. Brown) until I returned."

It seemed as if the water never would get hot. At last

Theoph, by deliberately scalding his hand in it, satisfied himself that it would "do," and was about to start off with a pailful, when a shrill scream caused him to spill half of it upon the floor.

"Help! Murder! Thieves!" screeched a voice from the sitting-room.

"Oh!" laughed Theoph, "it's Aunt Ann. Go quiet the poor soul, Em, while I call Kelly to take this pail."

In vain "Kelly, Kelly!" rang out on the midnight air. No individual of that name made his appearance. Theoph told me afterward, that when in desperation he carried the hot water to the barn himself, he found Kelly on his knees, hugging old Charley most affectionately.

"Ah, my honey!" whispered Kelly confidentially to Charles, "but we've had the fine time thegither. It's long since I've had a drop like that to warrum me. By Saint Pater! but whiskey's the stuff for a boy, anyhow!"

"You've been at the whiskey, have you? you scoundrel!" exclaimed Theoph, lifting the demijohn, and shaking it with unexpected facility. "Come, get up! Do you hear?"

"Have I bin at the whiskey, yer honor?" replied Kelly indignantly, as he raised his head from Charley's neck. "Och! is it dhrinkin' I would be, an' the poor baste a-dyin'?" and Charley received another hug.

Theophilus may have had great trials during the remainder of that night. I do not doubt it. But that was no reason why he should have been so fearfully cross all the next day. Kelly was a model of penitence, and promised by all the saints on the calendar never to transgress again; "exceptin'," he added, "I'm left all alone twicet

forninst a dimmyjohn wid the corrik out — and St. Patrick
himself couldn't howld out agin' the like o' that."

Charley did not die — not a bit of it.   He was only, as
his groom said, "a little overdid."   In a few days he was
quite himself again; and, before the week was over, I was
tempted to travel *en voiture* to the village once more.

I am happy to say our steed quite redeemed himself on the occasion.   The only fright he gave me was in
showing decided symptoms of lying down while Kelly was
in the feed-store.   To my great relief, a good-natured
negro boy came to the rescue.

After tugging a while at Charley's head, and giving him
a mouthful of water, he volunteered a remark or two: —

"Dat yere horse is weak, Miss Brown, he is — can't
har'ly stan' up — dat's a fac, he can't — 'pears to me dey
ort ter gib him more ter eat."

This was a little too much.   As I had no other audience,
I ventured to inform the sable youth that the animal had
always more food offered him than he would take.

"Den he wants powders.   Juss let dem gib him 'dition
powders fur de ap'tite: dey'd fotch him up mighty
quick."

The result of this little dialogue was, that before long
we purchased a package of Hadley's famous Condition
Powders.   Young Africa was right.   They *did* give Charley
an appetite.   He became ravenous as a wolf; but not an
ounce of fat appeared in consequence.   As Kelly face-
tiously remarked, it was "a race with him, whether to get
higher in the bone or lower in the flesh."   Even Bridget
had her joke at his expense, and talked of borrowing him
for a washboard.   Theophilus grumbled, and declared that

it cost more to feed him than it would to keep a span of ordinary horses ; and finally I announced, that ride behind his miserable carcass, I never, never would again.

Abandoning, therefore, all hope of using him for the present, his afflicted owner, paying well for the privilege, had him turned loose every day in an adjoining field. Theoph even examined the fences himself, to be certain that they were all secure ; for he had just received a letter from his dear Dobbs, alluding to "old Charley" in affectionate terms.

Here the creature's first exploit was to deliberately rush upon a broken rail, and injure himself so badly that we were obliged to send for a horse-doctor. Accordingly Kelly was despatched on foot to a small brick house in the village, proclaiming itself, by sundry signs, to be the abode of one Sanders, veterinary surgeon, and also of one Amos Dodd, who made and repaired gentlemen's clothing in the neatest possible style.

It was mournful, after all, to see Kelly riding back with the "docther" in a muddy gig, and to watch them standing near old Charley in solemn consultation. I felt as if there were a death in the family already. Dr. Sanders, however, bound up the injured leg, administered a pill of about the shape and size of the end of a potato-masher, and proclaimed his patient out of danger.

But no : Charles keeled over during the afternoon, and lay upon the grass whizzing like a capsized locomotive. Theophilus used some inelegant expressions while gazing upon him, and sent for Dr. Sanders again. After that, the hot mashes that Kelly was forced to prepare in the kitchen (especially on baking-days), the calls for flannel,

4*

Castile soap, rags, and hot water, to say nothing of the "dimmyjohn," were enough to drive a woman wild. At last Charles grew better. His wounds began to heal. Kelly tethered him in the very centre of the field, and went about his work whistling, until one day, when that sorely-tried individual ran up to the house in high wrath.

"Ah, Mr. Brown, sir, would ye come look at the horris! — whatever it is is the matter wid his leg, bad luck to it! It's bladin' worse ner ever, sir."

Surely enough: Charles, feeling something itching unmercifully, and having no finger-nails, had used his teeth with effect. Dr. Sanders swore when he looked at him.

"That 'ere horse needs knockin' on the head more'n any thing else," he observed.

"I can't do that," answered Theoph bitterly: "he's the gift of a friend."

"Friend be d——!" was the irreverent comment. "*I* wouldn't give such a creetur as that standing-room."

To make a long story short, Charles repeated the biting process so often, that Dr. Sanders declared it wasn't any use for him to be running on this fool's-errand business any longer; he couldn't do any good to the beast unless he had him down to his own place.

Theophilus was only too glad to have the patient removed; and Flowery Grove was accordingly relieved of his presence *pro tem.*

It was now late in August. Philly was getting on so well, all things considered, that our physician recommended us to remain out of town as long as practicable.

Poor Theoph did so hate those long walks to and from the station! Still, with mental reservations, we quite agreed with Miss Kimso that the country would be delightful when the melancholy days were come,

"The brownest of the year."

Meantime, letters came from Mr. Dobbs that filled the heart of Theophilus with delight.

"Dobbs would be comfortable, rich, in less than two years," he said; and he shouldn't be surprised, either, from certain indications, if the scamp had formed an attachment down there, or rather if he were hopelessly "smitten;" for there had not been time for any thing deliberate. "It is strange, too," he added, "that he does not reply to a solitary point in any of my letters. Oh, the rascal is surely in love!"

The conclusion of Mr. Dobbs's last letter, received in the autumn splendor, left no room for doubt.

"I shall start for New York by the next steamer," he wrote, "for a short stay only. California must be my home for some years to come. And, Brown, old boy, I shall not start *alone*. The loveliest, sweetest, dearest woman that God ever made will accompany me as my wife. We sailed out here in the same vessel, have known each other ever since, and — well, wait until you see her, that's all. Then, if you have any fault to find, fire away!

"If you are still at 'Flowery Grove' (ha, ha!), and you can get a room for us at good Miss Kimso's, we shall be most happy to give you a week of our delightful company immediately after landing. By the way, old chap, why don't you write? Not a line from you have I received. Ruggles & Co. have turned out *prime*.

"Pat old Charley for me, and (beg her pardon for the juxtaposition, but love for that horse is my weak spot) present my warmest remembrances to your dear wife. She will love my Annie, I know. Adieu! Pray for your Benedict.   Yours,   DOBBS."

"He will be here in ten days!" cried Theoph blissfully,

as he folded the letter; "and here comes Miss Kimso. Now we can speak about the room."

Miss Kimso assented to the plan very cheerfully, though it was with great difficulty that we could prevail upon her to accept any remuneration.

"What!" she cried. "'Is thy servant a dog, that she should do this thing?' 'Take the wandering stranger in,' and then charge him so much a week? Never!"

But it was satisfactorily arranged at last; and, as we all sat chatting on the piazza, I could not help observing how really pretty Miss Kimso was at times, especially when a look of peculiar brightness came to her eye, and some sudden emotion sent color to her cheek.

Theophilus was expatiating upon the virtues of his adorable Dobbs for our benefit, when Dr. Sanders, driving by in his dingy-looking gig, stopped to shout, —

"Mr. Brown, you'd better send for that horse of yourn. He's just eating his head off where he is."

"Eating his head off!" shrieked Miss Kimso, ready to believe any thing of old Charley. I explained to her the meaning of the phrase, while Theoph called out, —

"I'll send the man around this evening. And, Sanders, just let him have your bill at the same time, will you?"

"All right!" shouted the horse-doctor, as he drove off, leaving a cloud of dust behind him.

When Kelly brought old Charley home that evening, looking more bony and rickety than ever, and delivered the bill, I really was afraid Theophilus would say something wrong, he looked so desperate for an instant; but he evidently restrained himself.

"Eating his head off!" he exclaimed at last, after gazing upon the startling bit of paper. "Better say eaten the whole of his wretched carcass again and again. I wish Dobbs's mother would come and take her own!"

Just then I heard Nelly crying; and Miss Kimso, complaining of chilliness, bade me good 'evening, and ran home.

All that night I was restless. Perhaps it was because old Charley, ill at ease after his long absence, neighed more drearily than usual. Perhaps it was the memory of Theoph's unwonted fit of temper. Certain it is, I could not sleep a wink. The room was insufferably warm, though it was autumn; and two impish mosquitoes, the last of their race, tormented me to desperation. Finally, enveloped in a light shawl, I seated myself by the open window, and watched the fleckered moonlight as it lay trembling under our pear-tree. Sultry as was the air within, a light breeze was stirring out of doors, and the bright moon overhead seemed creeping slowly in and out among the clouds. Suddenly an unusually dismal neigh startled me, and looking toward the barn I saw something that made my very blood run cold.

Old Charley was walking slowly from the stable, and he was not alone! Gliding in advance, as though leading him by an invisible halter, was a tall white figure, pointing with outstretched finger toward the west. The face was turned away; but, with a gasp of horror, I noticed that the hair falling over its shoulder was scant and gray. The words of Theophilus flashed upon me, —

"*I wish that Dobbs's mother would come and take her own!*" With a shriek I flew toward the bed.

Theoph sprang up in an instant.

"Emma, my darling, what is it?"

"The GHOST!" I cried. "Dobbs's mother!" and fell fainting to the floor.

The entire household, as I afterward learned, was soon around me; and, while the servants were shuddering over my incoherent exclamations, Theoph hastened to explore the premises. That I had seen *something* was evident; but even Theophilus was not prepared for the phantom that stood with glittering eyes, to receive him as he opened the front door. In one skinny hand it held the halter that had been invisible to me, while over its shoulder the eyeballs of old Charley glared upon him with blank, remorseless stare.

Recovering his self-possession, Theoph seized the phantom by the arm.

"Good heavens, Miss Kimso!" he exclaimed, "what are you doing here? Are you ill?"

She awoke with a scream, and dropped the halter like one bewildered. As he led her back to her own house, he could see that something was wrong. She called him Albert, and clung, weeping, to his arm; and when he told her he was not Albert, but her neighbor and friend, she broke into a rattling laugh, and tried to get away from him.

She was better the next day, and in her own little room gave me the sad story of her life. I shall not repeat it here; but I did not wonder, when with tearless eye she told me that she had conquered herself, and ceased to look forward to Albert's return, that sometimes her outraged nature had vent in temporary delirium. These attacks, according to the account given by her faithful servant, were growing less and less frequent every year. Indeed, the doctor had said she might outlive them entirely.

The doctor was right: Miss Kimso began to grow stronger soon after the night of her somnambulic walk, when the moonlight silvered her floating brown hair, and transfigured her into an aged ghost. Black Phœbe helped us to account for the improvement, however, when one day she said confidentially, "It sartinly is won'ful strange now to think how Massa Albert is a comin' back, just his-self agin, as sorry and good as ever you see, an' ready to die for missus."

His first letter reached her on the very day that Mr. Dobbs returned ; and the dear little woman was radiant with happiness. A soft light beamed in her eyes, though the quotations came thick and fast as ever.

As for Mr. Dobbs's wife, she was certainly a charming young person. We were friends from the very first. It was such a relief to see somebody else besides Theophilus worshipping Mr. Dobbs !

Before they had been with us an hour, we were all, including Miss Kimso, clustered together near the porch, laughing and chatting like old friends.

Suddenly the countenance of Theophilus assumed a sardonic grin.

"Dobbs," said he, "I'm going to do something hand-some. From this hour old Charley is yours again. Accept him as a wedding-gift to yourself and lovely young bride."

Mr. Dobbs stammered forth his thanks, and declared he would be "right glad to see the noble old fellow again."

"Let the noble old fellow be brought forth!" com-manded Theoph in a tragic voice.

Kelly soon appeared, dragging the wedding-gift after him by main force.

Mr. Dobbs sprang to his feet.

"That's not old Charley!" he cried, as soon as his emotions would allow him to articulate. "That's" — And the gentleman doubled himself up with laughter.

"It *is* old Charley, though," returned Theoph positively.

"I tell you it is not," gasped Mr. Dobbs. "It's — oh, dear, I shall die! — it's a horse that I sold long ago to Jim Fowler, over in Westchester County, for fifteen dollars!"

Theoph turned red, rushed into the house, and soon came out again with a crumpled sheet of paper.

Mr. Dobbs seized it, and read aloud, —

J. FOWLER.

Dear Sir, — Wishing to have my old horse again, I enclose forty dollars, which, I believe, covers every thing. Please deliver him to bearer, and (to prevent mistake) return this letter with your receipt by same hand. In haste,

Yours, respectfully, CHARLES G. DOBBS.

"That's straight enough, sir, isn't it?" exclaimed Theoph triumphantly. "Kelly brought it back with him on that same day ; and here's the receipt. — Kelly!"

"Yez, sir."

"Didn't you get this horse from Mr. Fowler?"

"Sure, sir, I did," began Kelly ; "and" —

"Of course he did!" interrupted Mr. Dobbs. "They're all named 'Fowler' in that part of the country. But it was *John* Fowler that had old Charley, not *James*. By the way," he continued, drawing a package from his vest-pocket,

"I have brought some unopened letters with me. There were such stacks of them waiting for me when I landed, that I've not had time to read half. Let's see. Ah, here we are! This looks like it." And he tore a yellow envelope asunder.

Mr. Dobbs.

Respected Sir [this is it, sure enough], — as your remittances have not come to hand since last April, I take the liberty to send my little account for your horse's board; which please to pay as soon as you can, as I have none too much on hand at present to settle my spring bills. Old Charley looks better now than any young horse in the place. He would fetch a price, if you could make up your mind to sell him. There's people asking me about him most every day. I've rented my house and stables, out and out, after this summer, but can get Charley in prime selling order in two weeks. Excuse me for asking, but I do wish I knew why you sent Jim Fowler, down the road, forty dollars for that old nag of his. It was twenty-five dollars more than he give you for him.

Please settle the enclosed bill as soon as you can, and oblige

Your obedient servant, JOHN FOWLER.

By the time Mr. Dobbs ceased reading, Theophilus was quite prepared to appreciate the joke. In fact, we all laughed: Kelly roared; and even old Charley (?), who stood near, threw up his head, and made a sound wonderfully like ha! ha!

Theophilus spoke first.

"Dobbs," said he, "I have a proposition to make. There is an unpaid bill in this pocket, from the horse-doctor who has attended yonder steed through various slight ailments. You must have a pretty big one for your Charley's board. We both are ignorant of their amounts. What say you to a blind exchange? Will you do it?" and he held out the folded bill at arm's-length.

Mr. Dobbs glanced once more at John Fowler's "little

5

account." Then he put his hands into his pockets, and gave one long, penetrating look at "old Charley."

Finally he looked up. "No, Brown," said he solemnly: "I couldn't do it. Upon my soul, I couldn't."

After this, Charley drooped; and what wonder? His days were numbered; though, as his groom assured us, he kept his "faculties" to the last.

"Arrah, sir," Kelly would say, "it would do yer harrit good to see the crayture, wid his old ways on him as strong and fresh now: ye'd be astonished. Faith, it's balkin' he often is, a-shtandin' there in his shtall, wid never a sowl urgin' him, at all, at all. Ye can see by the looks of him that he's just tuk it int' his head not to shtir anudder shtep, though it's shtandin' shtill he's bin all the time. An' to see the bones of him! Och, but it's comin' through his insides they are, since they cuddn't stick out no furder. Is it oats, or carrits? Arrah! the more ye fatten him, the thinner he gits. Bad luck to the day I fetched him!"

Poor old Charley! Even Mr. Dobbs soon stopped laughing at him. He did not die after the usual manner of horses, but slowly shrivelled away; and, before we went to town, we laid him tenderly under our pear-tree.

PHILLY AND THE REST.

THEOPHILUS and I had quite a discussion the other night, concerning our Philly.

Philly is a good boy, and a healthy boy. He's straight as an arrow, and would know a hawk from a hernshaw as quickly as any one, if those two birds were in the habit of flying daily before his dear little nose. But Theophilus thinks that when a youngster gets to be six years old, and not only is unacquainted with his letters, but evinces a decided unwillingness to learn them, it is time for the parents to look at each other, and ask, "Is this our child a fool?"

Theoph generally is in the right; but he certainly is unduly anxious about Philly. Any one would suppose, to hear him talk, that the dear child should by this time be able to recite half of Webster's Unabridged with his eyes shut — just as if he wouldn't be an unbearable little prig if he could! For my part, I love him all the more for his dear, stupid little ways. He'll come out all right in time. It's delightful to hear him try to count, "*one, three, five, two, seven*" — bless his heart! But Theophilus always looks grave and troubled at these attempts, and tries

to teach him the proper sequence.   Philly listens for a
moment ; but what can one do with him ? . He has a
way of wriggling under a lesson, that soon forces one to
kiss his rosy, laughing little cheeks, and let him go.   Ah !
you should have seen Theophilus just after the discussion
I have alluded to.   Half in fun, and half because I was
provoked at him for his solemn way of taking Philly, I
took up a book, and began to read aloud a life of the
wonderful child Candiac : —

" ' Candiac, John L. de Montcalm [I began impressively], a child of wonderfully precocious talents, was a brother of the Marquis de Montcalm who was
killed at the battle of Quebec.   He was born in 1719 ; and at three years of
age read French and Latin fluently.' "

Theophilus sighed ; but I proceeded without noticing
it, —

" ' When four years old he had mastered arithmetic ; and, before seven sum-
mers had passed over his head, he had acquired Hebrew, Greek, heraldry,
geography, and much of fabulous and sacred and profane history.' "

Theoph almost groaned.   I continued, —

" ' His extraordinary acquirements were a theme of panegyric to many
literary characters of that age.' "

"Seven years," moaned Theoph, — "only one year older
than our Philly !   Dear me ! what an astonishing child !
Go on, dear : what else did he do ? "

"What else *could* he do," I rejoined severely, "but
die ? Here, read it for yourself.   Born in 1719, and died
of hydrocephalus in 1726."

" Oh ! " said Theoph.

" Ah, here is another ! " I said, peering into the book ;
"shall I read it ? "

" Certainly, my love."

" ' The annals of precocity present no more remarkable instance than the brief career of Christian Heinecker, born at Lubeck, Feb. 6, 1721. At the age of ten months he could speak, repeating every word that was said to him ; when twelve months old, he knew by heart the principal events narrated in the Pentateuch ; in his second year he learned the greater part of the history of the Bible, both of the Old and New Testaments ; in his third year he could reply to most questions on universal history and geography, and in the same year he learned to speak Latin and French ; in his fourth year he employed himself in the study of religion and the history of the Church ; and he was able not only to repeat what he had read, but also to reason upon it, and express his own judgment. The King of Denmark wishing to see this wonderful child, he was taken to Copenhagen, there examined before the court, and proclaimed a wonder.' "

" Tremendous ! " exclaimed Theoph, " but very unnatural. Still I must say I would be glad to have a child like that."

" Would you ? " I responded dryly, casting a glance of suppressed indignation toward the crib where dear little Philly lay asleep. " But I've not read it all yet."

" Ah ! excuse me, love."

" ' This account of him by his teachers is confirmed by many respectable contemporary authorities. On his return home from Copenhagen he learned to write ; but his constitution being weak, he shortly after fell ill.' "

" Ah ! got sick, did he ? I believe that *is* the way often with these extraordinary children. Probably he remained always sickly — but I beg pardon, go on."

" No, Theoph," I answered, in a low but awful tone, " he did not remain ill at all. He died then and there, at the age of four years and four months."

" Oh ! " said Theoph again.

In a few moments he rose and crossed the room. I
13*

knew he was bending over Philly; but I didn't look up from the book.

"Come here, dear," he said at last.

I obeyed. Well, it *was* strange. There lay our fair-browed little boy, rosy and dewy with sleep; one adventurous little bare foot was thrust out from beneath the soft blanket; his left hand tightly held a slate-pencil; the other, with chubby finger extended, was pointing to a slate that lay on the coverlet beside him; and on this slate was a great big A, which Theoph had drawn upon it that afternoon, now criss-crossed all over with Philly's pencil-marks.

"He really does appear to be pointing at it," I said, in rather an awed voice.

"We'll take it for a sign," added Theoph quietly. "We wont trouble the little chap with books yet a while. Plenty of time for that sort of thing when he's older."

Then he leaned over the crib, and laid his cheek close to Philly's; and, as I thought it best not to make any remark, I went back to the table and took up my sewing.

Now the two children, Candiac and Heinecker, were extreme instances of precocity, I admit. But we sometimes need extreme instances to point a moral, and especially in convincing a person like Theoph, who holds on to an opinion with all his might, forcing you to do the same; and then, just as you are trusting your whole weight to the obstinacy of his argument, it snaps like an overtaxed rope, leaving you, as I may say, a prostrate victor. When he gives in, he does it so completely that you've nothing to say, and must just sit in silence, letting your unuttered arguments seethe within you till you cool off.

I might have reminded him of the wonderful boyhood

of Pascal, who found mathematics in his porridge, and who was forced, in his infantile pursuit of geometry, to call a circle a *round*, and a line a *bar*, because his wise father peremptorily withheld all book-knowledge of the subject from the precocious little one. Or I could have opened another biography, and read to him of Bossuet, "The Eagle of Meaux," as his eulogists have called him. This wonderful creature, when only eight years of age, preached with unction at the Hotel de Rambouillet. But, as we all know, he went on preaching, growing more and more able and eloquent as the years passed by, and died at last in a green old age. So his was not a citable case in my regard. It would have been much more to the point to dwell upon the dull boyhood of some of the world's most eminent men : of how Corneille was called a dunce by his schoolmaster ; of how Master Walter Scott was the blockhead of his class ; of how the poor, sickly schoolboy, Newton, was always in trouble on account of inattention ; and how impossible it was to make little Danny Webster speak his " piece " at school on declamation-days, — how that was the one thing he couldn't and wouldn't do, any more than Philly would learn his letters.

But Theoph might then have turned about and renewed the defence. He might have quoted, as he often had before, the childhood of Galileo, of whom some old frump has said ecstatically, that, "while other little ones of his age were whipping their tops, he was scientifically considering the cause of their motion." Very likely he would have thrown Dr. Johnson and Lord Jeffrey at me, both of whom are said to have been profoundly wise, even in their petticoats. Then there was the great Frenchman, Gassendi, who was only four years of age when the study of astronomy began to engross him; and Humphry Davy delivering scientific lectures to his nursery chairs; and Dr. Arnold, glad at the ripe age of three to be presented with Smollett's "History of England."

No, it was better as it was. A relapse of the argument might prove more formidable than the original attack.

Dear, good Theoph! What differences of opinion could ever come seriously between him and me? And yet, there *is* a great deal to be said on the subject of juvenile precocity; and, if he ever goes dangerously back to his old views about Philly, I shall have to say it. I'll tell him how direful a thing it nearly always is, this preternatural activity of the faculties. I'll read physiological essays to him; and I'll ask him whether, if he were to go out into his Long Island orchard on some mild day in March, and find an apple-tree fairly bubbling over with rapid blossoms, he would expect to find many apples on that tree when summer came. Of course he wouldn't.

Perhaps it would be a more philosophical way to put it, if I said, "How would you like your trees to pop forth early in the spring with full-grown fruit? Wouldn't you miss blossom-time? and wouldn't apples probably be all gone before Christmas?"

Surely we should regard with reverence the blossom-time of life. If we force it into premature fruitage, we shall be disappointed in the end. And how much we lose, if, in a slow, beautiful blossoming, we find not the exceeding joy that childhood brings to itself and to us!

Dwelling on my simile to illustrate another serious phase of the subject, I might ask Theoph how he would like to have the beautiful floral wonders stripped from his trees as soon as they appeared, and hung in fantastic garlands all about the outer limits of each branch. Yet that is precisely what those mistaken souls do who turn the simple, beautiful ways of their children into drawing-room displays; who catch at every bright little saying as soon as it leaves the infantile lips, and in the child's presence dangle it before admiring guests. Ah, the wrongs that are committed in this way, — the holy childish impulses that are sent back, despoiled, into the wondering, childish heart, there to wither to a little wisp of vanities! The sweet music that springs forth unconsciously at first, but in time halts in discords, because it has learned to wait for the perverted maternal echo!

Mothers, fathers — all who drink in happiness through the love you bear to little children — revere the freshness of a young nature. Don't, let your weak, doting admiration, or your still weaker pride of possession, put the blight of self-consciousness upon it. I'd rather see a child of mine playing with the molasses-jug, just after I had dressed the little one in its Sunday clothes, than to hear it speak, "My name is Norval," with the assurance of an infant prodigy. I'd almost rather it should have the measles as a chronic institution, than to see it ready at all times to display its *repertoire* of accomplishments before strangers. Luckily, little ones are not apt to fall into this latter accommodating habit. They rather protest with all their charming might against it.

"Isn't it always so?" exclaimed a mother in despairing tones the other day. "Can you *ever* get a child to show off when you wish it to?" And there sat her obdurate toddler, outwardly serene in its enjoyment of a candy bribe, which had stickied its little mouth and nose in a remarkable way, but all aflame with inward determination *not* to sing " Bobby Shaftoe." " It's too bad ! " cooed the mother: " you ought to hear him do it. He really has quite an ear for music, and his pronunciation is irresistible."

Now, " pronunciation " and " irresistible " might not have been quite as comprehensible terms to that baby as to the youthful Candiac or to Master Heinecker ; but there was one thing he could understand, and that was the unguarded admiration of his mother ; not her appreciation and love, — these would have sunk into his child-soul like nourishing dews, — but the admiration, that, falling too often on a young nature, blights it, or forces it to a premature and unnatural growth.

Philly knows little songs, and long ago he could say, —

" Who comes here ?   A grenadier ! "

but we always have been very careful how and when we brought forward these accomplishments. He knows that he can please us immensely by an exercise of his dramatic and musical gifts. ، Before he grew so old and wise, he believed that he frightened us terribly, when, in saying that thrilling nursery lyric, he roared forth, " *A granny-deer !*" but now he just knows that we enjoy his performances as he does ours ; and we always make a point of giving a fair exchange in such entertainments.

To be sure, if Philly, instead of being the simple, every-day child that he is, had proved to be an infant Mozart, with God-given genius shining from his eyes, and twitching his restless little fingers, of course we should feel in duty bound to lift him to the piano-stool. We would do this reverently, I think, and with joyful wonder ; glad, too, that the progress of science and the arts had prepared for our dear boy something better than a clavichord. We might even encourage him to put his music upon paper, if his overflowing soul required that form of expression. Or, premising that we had seen marvellous cows, elephants, and dogs chalked on the nursery doors, or on Philly's one-eyed and tailless hobby-horse ; or if, when he was six years old, another Lady Kenyon had walked in, and our precious little one had in half an hour drawn an excellent portrait of her, after the manner of the six-year-old Thomas Lawrence, does any one suppose that the maternal grasp would have robbed our boy's right hand of its cunning ?

But he's *not* a Mozart. He's not any thing in particular, though he's every thing to us. He simply represents " a large and growing class of the community," as the newspapers say ; and so his case is worthy of consideration. He's the average child (ah ! how it hurts my motherly heart to write that ; for it doesn't believe a word of it, though *I* do) ; and, being the average child, we all may learn a lesson from him for the benefit of the present race of little ones.

We can resolve, that, for him, all precocious development is hurtful: premature ability, premature politeness, premature pleasures, premature goodness even, — Heaven shield him from them all ! Heaven shield him and every other child from aught that will stiffen them too soon into little men and women !

I know three little tots, five and six years old, who lately have returned from a visit to Europe. One of these, under the modern hot-house plan of mental culture, has grown to be *such* an intelligent child, such a little lady !

I asked her the other day what she liked best of all she saw in Europe.

"Oh! the art-galleries, of course," she replied demurely : "everybody likes those best."

Poor child ! Remembering her, with what comfort I recall a recent morning spent with the two other little travellers.

"So you have been to Europe," I said. "Now, Hal, tell me what place did *you* like best of all ? "

"Don't know," said Hal : "guess I liked Munich best, 'cause they had the most sojers there."

"And I think I liked Venice," put in wee, bright-eyed May ; "because it was there that mamma bought me this sweet little doll " [taking it up caressingly]. "Her name's Katie. I must finish putting on her clothes : it's very late in the morning for dolly not to be all washed and dressed, I think. Ah ! " she continued plaintively, as she attempted to pin dolly's skirt, "this band is too big. Katie used to just fit it ; but she's real thin now, she's lost so much saw-dust ! "

Happy little May ! Her days are fresh and simple and beautiful, because she is allowed to be a child. Whatever training is expended upon her is so loving and wise, that she grows naturally into all that can be rationally expected of a child of her age. Her goodness is the goodness of a warm-hearted, unperverted little girl, who loves the dear God already "for making father and mother and every thing," but who has no startling Sunday-school predilec-tions, suggestive of an early transplanting. Her politeness comes from no formal schooling, but is the simple outgrowth of the "love one another" that comes of being loved, — not of being doted upon, but of being loved as God intended she should be.

May's pretty ways are in her presence never made the subject of admiring comment; nor are her sweet, childish sayings echoed by the mountains of appreciation with which children among the comfortable classes are so apt to be surrounded. If she asks a question, it is thoughtfully answered; and if she makes any of those sweet, childish blunders in speech or conduct that often are the charm of our homes, they either are apparently not noticed at all at the time, or they are gently and cheerfully corrected. But never are they met by that domestic dyke, in the form of a general laugh or an encouraging deception, which invariably sends them back upon the child in an overflow of pain or bewilderment.

The fondest of us parents often are the most cruel to our children. This comes from selfishly regarding them as an especial personal gift to ourselves, something to delight and amuse us; while at the same time we forget, that, if they are given to us, just as surely are we given to them.

As a general rule, we are not half thoughtful or courteous enough in our manners toward our little ones. We are too apt to content ourselves with a general consciousness of being right in the main, with theoretically intending that they shall grow up to be good Christian citizens, and an honor to ourselves. We make big sacrifices in their behalf, revolve fine schemes, and bring out the heavy artillery of our nature on very slight occasions. But our graces, our courtesies, our delicate acts of appreciation

and lofty consideration are not for them. These are re-
served for adult friends and select acquaintances, as if to
any one living were due more of the best and sweetest
that is in us than to those whom we have brought into the
world, to meet its jars, temptations, and cruelties.

Think of the really coarse way in which the best of
us sometimes wound our children's sensibilities. How we
parade their special traits and accomplishments, and
ignore their individuality; how recklessly we break in
upon their little plans and pleasures; how carelessly we
comment upon their defects ; how we laugh at their childish distresses, because the grieved look or the tragic little
scowl is "so cunning;" how we visit our vexation of
spirit upon their innocent heads ; how we resent their
inexperience; how needlessly or sharply we deny their
little petitions, and how we ignore *our* "Thank you," and
insist upon theirs ; how we jerk or push them in our
impatience ; how we flout their earnest questions, and deal
out cutting, cruel words of "wholesome reproof," when
perhaps the little heart is quivering under some real or
fancied wrong !   It is terrible to think of !

Many, seeing these charges in the aggregate, will indignantly deny them.   Yet what parent, answering each in
turn, could plead guiltless to them all ?

I shall not dwell upon the monstrous wrongs of chas-
tisement too often inflicted upon children, — such as beating, threatening, frightening, and that meanest act of all,
the "boxing" of ears.   The dear Christ teaches no hard
lesson of harshness or brute force toward the little ones
committed to our care.   Even as he was "subject unto"
his parents, returning meekly with them from Jerusalem

while his child-soul yearned to be about his Father's business, so would he have our little ones subject unto us.
They are ours to lead and protect, to teach and warn and
cherish ; ours to love wisely, to deal with firmly and reverently, — mirrors of our example, gleaners of the harvest
of our home-life, — not ours to humor and rebuff, and
sacrifice to our hundred weaknesses. Well for the father
and mother to whom their child's heart is as a holy of
holies ; and their child's foibles and human tendencies as
stumbling-blocks, not to vex and upset parents, but which
the little one must wisely and lovingly be taught to overcome. Heaven bless the always cheerful, gentle-voiced, conscientious parent ! And Heaven help all those, who, when
it is too late to atone, remember with anguish the quivering
lip and pleading look of a little face that has passed away !

Mothers, when in your hearts rises that first blessed
thought, God has given to me a child, then and there say,
" O child ! He has given me to thee. He has chosen me
to be thy mother."

Then, with His help, shall your little one be reared. No
selfish fondness nor pride shall rob it of its just rights ;
not a tithe shall be taken from its innocent, sweet babyhood, from its growing infancy, its blithesome childhood.
Sufficient unto each day shall be its daily progress. Van-
ity shall not warp it, nor school-books crush, nor undue
stimulus wrong it of its fair and just proportions.

When you say, with the woman of old, "Lo, I have
given a man unto the world," be guarded lest you cheat it,
and Heaven too, by not allowing that man first to be, in
the fullest sense, a little child.

OUR AGGY.

———◆———

ADVISABLE, Mrs. Winthrop!" I exclaimed, "advisable! Why, it is a clear case of duty! If no one else can be induced to take the poor girl, I will assume the responsibility myself, though I have three servants already."

Mrs. Winthrop, a Bostonian, of "Mayflower" descent, who had only lately entered our New York set, and who was considerate and deferential accordingly, gave an admiring start, and suggested her fear that ."The creature would drive me wild."

"I have no such apprehension," was my lofty reply: "kindness and firmness must inevitably overcome the most refractory natures. Besides, the child may not be half as bad as Mrs. Grimmons imagines."

Mrs. Winthrop inclined her head slightly toward her left shoulder, and, as if yielding to an irresistible internal flood of argument, ejaculated (for the twentieth time during our morning's conversation), "Yes-s !?"

And here allow me to relieve myself concerning this inexplicable Boston "Yes." It cannot be written ; and I defy the most skilful printer, by means of any complica-

tion of italics, dashes, or notes of interrogation or exclamation, to express it in all its fulness, its provokingness.
It is yielding, defiant, coaxing, snubbing, conciliatory, and
threatening, all in a breath. It is susceptible of every
shade of meaning, of almost every slang reply that one
can hear from the Atlantic to the Pacific. It says, "Just
so," and "You can't come it over me!" "Go it, my
hearty!" and "A leetle tough!" "What a whopper!"
and "Them's my sentiments!" "Go it blind!" "Aren't
you stretching it?" "Bully for you!" "Hit 'em again!"
"No, yer don't!" and "Sartain now!"   And all the time
it is so Bostonianly elegant that one must wince under it
with folded hands, and take its meaning as one best can.

Mrs. Winthrop's "*Yes-s!?*" meant a great deal, and I
knew it.

In the first place, it meant, "You think so, do you?"
Second, "I hardly think you can succeed where the intel-
lectual Mrs. Grimmons failed; but who can tell?" Third,
"What a conceited woman you are if you only knew it!"
Fourth, "You are entirely wrong; but you must find it
out in the regular way." And Fifth, "Well, we're fortunate, at least, in getting the girl temporarily off our
hands."

Taking in all this with my usual acumen, I cut the matter short with, —

"You will please inform the ladies of my resolve, Mrs.
Winthrop, as I cannot attend the sewing-meeting to-day.
They may send the girl to me on Monday morning if she
is not otherwise disposed of by that time."

"I shall do so," rejoined my visitor, rising gracefully
from the sofa. "And now, my dear friend, when may we
hope to see you and your good husband at No. 69?"

"Very soon, thank you," I answered, throwing aside my business air; "on the first evening, in fact, when I can succeed in enticing Mr. Brown from his library chair. How is your little Everett, Mrs. Winthrop?"

"Oh! nicely, thank you. He and Annie are attending school now. Do allow your little ones to visit them on Saturdays. Your Julie is so charming and well-behaved that I should really admire to have Annie become intimate with her."

I assured Mrs. Winthrop, who, whatever may be her peculiarities, has certainly fine instincts where children are concerned, that I considered Julie quite too young to leave "mother" yet.

"Yes-s!?" returned Mrs. Winthrop musingly, adding, in a more sprightly tone, "but cannot 'mother' come also?"

By this time the door was reached; and, after many a pleasant smile and nod and half-heard sentence on both sides, we parted, the lady's elegant skirts sweeping down the stone steps, while I mounted slowly and thoughtfully to the nursery, feeling morally sure that "the creature" would make her appearance on Monday.

Yes, morally sure. All the rest of that day I kept asking myself, *à la Bulwer*, "What will I do with her?" And next, the married woman's watchword, "What will *He* say?" came forcibly to mind. Poor Theophilus! my faultless, ease-loving, propriety-worshipping master of the house! What would he say, indeed? I trembled to think of it. Why, even Ann McNamara, our peerless cook, had narrowly escaped being "dismissed" by him the day before, just because she had served the *ragout* in an unsuitable dish; and Bettys and Biddys innumerable had been banished from our domicile for the most petty offences against his fastidious taste. Probably we should not by this time have had a servant in the house, had I not, a few weeks before, "taken a stand" in rather a decided manner. Yes, the small-failings question had been then and there settled between us for all time. Thenceforth no girl who suited *me* should share the fate of my sainted highly respectable ones of the past. But could my new girl, my *rara avis*, take shelter under the statute? I had seen her, and knew, or fancied I knew, what was before me. But Theophilus!

Well, the only way was to put a bold face on the matter. Accordingly, as the shades of evening approached, I summoned all my forces, and prepared to meet his lordship. Under the circumstances, his first salutation was not encouraging.

"Emma, dear, judging from appearances, one would suppose Mary's usual way of laying the door-mat was to fling it from the second-story window. I am afraid she never will be tidy enough to suit us."

"I fear so too," I replied amiably; for a bright idea had just struck me. "The fact is, Theophilus, it is impossible to teach these 'competent' help any thing. What we really want is a raw girl."

"A what! Emma?" exclaimed Theophilus, horror-stricken, as, after placing his boots with mathematical accuracy near the polished register, he stood with arrested slipper in each hand.

"A raw girl; one that is not hopelessly set in other people's ways, — that, — in short, — one that is, as you may say, — ignorant, but willing to learn," said I sweetly, giving his elegant "wrapper" a caressing shake as I handed it to him.

"A Castle-Garden emigrant, for instance, newly-landed, or a blushing Huyter-spluyter fresh from the Vaterland?" suggested Theophilus, with intense humor, as he softly slid himself into the gown, and assumed his waiting-for-dinner attitude before the fire.

"No, no!" I laughed nervously, "nothing of that sort; but, ahem!" — as if the idea had just flashed upon me — "what do you say, now, Theoph, to my trying a colored girl?"

Theophilus either was speechless, or did not choose to reply; and I proceeded, —

"Not one of those deceitful, half-and-half yellow kind, that are neither one thing nor the other, but a genuine negress. They're generally such docile-tempered creatures, you know, Theoph; and, nowadays, it really seems to be a Christian duty to"—

"Christian fiddlestick!" interrupted Theophilus profanely. "Why, Emma, you're crazy!" And my gentleman significantly consulted his watch.

Remembering at this critical moment the advice of the ancient philosopher concerning hungry men, I adjourned at once to the dining-room, and there held a session of great length and brilliancy, which, it is needless to add, resulted in the total subjugation of the refractory member. What I said, or what I did not say, can not be detailed here. Oh! the arguments I was forced to drive into that man before he admitted what by this time had grown to positive conviction with me; viz., that to have a real

Southern negro in our house, all things considered, was one of the greatest blessings that could befall us.

All this happened long ago, during war-times. I had learned this poor slave-girl's history at our last society-meeting. She and her father had escaped from Virginia into the Union lines. Theoretically a welcome had been shown them ; but practically the girl had, by her insubordination and impishness, proved too much for their hospitality, and a unanimous ticket-of-leave had soon been voted her. Two young soldiers coming Northward had, out of pity for the good old father, brought him and his child to New York, and presented them to our Ladies' Soldiers' Aid Society.

The old man was soon disposed of; but the girl, ah ! there was the rub. One by one impulsive members courageously gave her a trial ; but at each weekly meeting the despairing mistresses would in turn restore her to the bosom of the Society, declaring that they could do nothing with her. No direct charges were made ; and all that one could gather from the exclamations and complaints usually vented on these occasions, was that the girl had proved to be " queer," " forlorn," " unmanageable," and " awful," — singular qualities, certainly, in one who had worked in the fields all her young life, who had never known a mother's care, and to whom all womanly and household duties were sealed mysteries.

Meantime the strange creature would stand in a corner of the fine parlor, rolling her great dark eyes about, glancing from the company to the ceiling, and from the ceiling to the floor, in quick flashes of white and black, her hands folded meekly before her, with now and then a restless movement of her feet that invariably caused the ladies near her to start in spite of themselves. Sometimes, while looking the image of mute despair, she would suddenly clap her hands upon her knees, and burst into a sputtering laugh, only to appear more solemn than ever the next instant.

She was about fifteen years of age, and the blackest of the black. Her dress was a scant blue calico skirt, reaching nearly to the ankles, over which a long crash bib was drawn without a fold from neck to knee. Each temple was adorned with a few stiffly-plaited spikes emerging from the luxuriant wool; and her feet were covered with good new shoes and stockings, very much against her will, as it subsequently proved.

"Why not take the child myself?" I had thought, while sitting near her corner at the last meeting, and fancying I could detect a promise in her face of something better than she had yet chosen to display to her Northern friends. But the scheme had soon been abandoned as impracticable, and probably never would have recurred to me had not Mrs. Winthrop, during her morning call, suggested, in her non-committal way, that it was "advisable" a home should be found for the poor creature.

Theophilus, as I have already intimated, had been brought to that state of mind so often attained by the acquiescing Barkis. Still the work of preparation was not complete. Our last nurse had contrived to smuggle into the nursery a story of a "big black nigger," who thought nothing of gobbling down naughty boys and girls. Her hearers, strong in faith, had listened and believed; and, ever since, negroes in general, and his sable cannibalship in particu-

lar, had been the terror of their young lives. Of the chil
dren, young Theophilus (though it may be unwomanly
and quite out of my sphere for me to say so) was a greater
coward than either of the girls. He was afraid of his own
shadow. A dark room was fuller to him than Madame
Tussaud's Chamber of Horrors. Once he locked himself
in a pantry, and screamed till he fell almost into a convul-
sion before it occurred to him to unlock the door and come
out. These I mention merely as slight psychological
peculiarities. Being our only son, his father and I centred
our fondest hopes in him.

' Well, what poor little Philly would do or say when my
"contraband" should appear I couldn't imagine. Meantime, however, I resolved to clarify his ideas somewhat on
the negro question, and trust to fate for the result. As
for Julie and Nelly, they soon became sound to the core
on the subject; but I dreaded to think of the effect of that
woolly head and those great rolling eyes upon the baby.
So much for upstairs.

On Sunday morning I descended to the kitchen while
Theophilus was preparing to shave. Ann was there in full
glory. It was her Sunday out ; and her winter style set
off her portly figure to advantage. The instant my foot
crossed the door-sill I could not resist a secret recognition
of her local supremacy. Nora soon came in with the
coal-scuttle, and crinoline twice as extensive as my own ;
while Ellen, conscious of her unimpeachability as first-class
waitress, was washing dishes in the corner. Now was the
time to strike the final blow. In a few feeling words I
told my assembled audience the story of the poor "contraband." They heard me in silence, preferring, as usual,

to defer comment until they had the kitchen entirely to themselves. Finally I plunged into the catastrophe, and went on swimmingly, until arrested by Ann's indignant outburst, —

"Och! is it take the dirrity crayture yerself, yer mane, ma'am?"

"Certainly," I returned firmly, "if no one shelters her or teaches her to work, the poor girl must perish in the streets."

"An' it's what I never did, ma'am, slape and ate wid nagers; an' I'll not be afther beginnin' it now. So, if ye plaze, ma'am, ye'll be engagin' another cook agen me month's up."

Nora said nothing; and Ellen, after swinging into the pantry with a tray full of china, came out with a lofty, —

"I'd like to be lavin' with Ann, too, ma'am."

Here was a fine dilemma! But I was determined to carry out my project.

"You need neither eat nor sleep with her: she can take her meals at a side-table, and use the small garret-room. The girl is coming to-morrow; and I intend that she shall be treated kindly."

With these words I strode majestically from the kitchen, giving no token of the sinking at my heart: not even when I reached the dressing-room, except by shutting the door after me so violently that Theophilus, I regret to say, cut his chin.

On Monday morning we were startled by the most terrific yells and screams that ever mortal parents heard. Theophilus rushed first; I followed, quite sure that Mr.

Norris's bull-dog had got in from the next yard, and was crunching every one of dear little Philly's bones.

Arriving at the turn of the stairs, we saw at a glance that our boy was safe and sound, though screaming in an agony of terror. His little sisters were with him in the hall, both talking at once, trying to bring him to reason; while Ann, Ellen, and Nora were on the spot, "speaking their minds" at concert pitch.

Meanwhile the innocent cause of all this commotion stood near the hat-stand, with a half-doleful, half-mischievous expression of countenance, her hands plucking nervously at the fringe of her coarse shawl, and her whole aspect betokening either amusement or distress, it was impossible to decide which.

"Mrs. Grimmons's boy left her here, ma'am. She wouldn't sit, nor go up stairs nor down," whispered Nora, hurrying toward me. "The child was frightened into fits, indeed he was, ma'am, at the very sight of her."

Philly was soon high and safe in his father's arms, being lectured and hugged at the same time. Without replying to Nora, I nodded to the new-comer, saying with my usual dignity, as I led the way to the room at the end of the hall, "Step this way, please."

On reaching the door, a suppressed giggle from the top of the kitchen-stair caused me to turn. The maiden by the hat-stand had not budged an inch.

"Will you come this way, please?" I repeated kindly, in a louder tone.

No answer and no movement. The children, seeing fun ahead, fairly danced with delight.

"Behave yourselves, children!" I commanded. "There,

7

the baby is awake: run up, Nora!—Now, my girl," re
suming my bland tone, "just come this way, will you?"

Was she marble, or, more properly speaking, ebony?
Her immovability was scarcely human.

At this juncture Theophilus, whose manner never
seemed to me half so impressive as my own, caught her
eye.   He pointed to the room-door.   The girl darted
through the hall, and stood beside me in an instant, her
lithe frame all in a quiver.

"Don't be frightened, my child," I said gently, feeling
really sorry for the poor creature : "no one here will harm
you.   What is your name?"

"Nuffin," she replied, with a sulky pout.

"You certainly must have some name.   What did the
soldiers call you?"

"Nig."

"What else?"

"Nuffin' else, 'cept 'fractory an' debbil."

"But your father, what does *he* call you?"

"What he call me?   He call me gal."

"Nothing else?"

"Nuffin', 'cept when I'se sick er bin whipt: den he call
me Aggy."

"Aggy's your name, then.   Was that your mother's
name?"

"What say, missy?" with a blank stare.

"Was your mother's name Aggy?"

"'Spect not; 'spect I didn't hab no mudder.   I'se
gwine;" and with these words Miss Aggy turned, and
started resolutely for the door.

Theophilus stepped nimbly in advance of her, locked it,

and put the key into his pocket. From that moment he was her acknowledged master.

The breakfast-bell rang. "Aggy," said I, not wishing to consign her yet to the tender mercies of the help, "come back and sit down."

She obeyed.

"Don't leave this room until I return."

"No, missy."

I gave one penetrating look at the girl, and saw that she was in earnest. Mustering the children (Philly was long ago safely perched upon the kitchen table), we descended to the basement.

Theophilus behaved pretty well at breakfast, considering; merely hinting that I should have my hands full, and that firmness must be the order of the day, as if I didn't know that already.

Suddenly he broke out with one of his speeches.

"I say, Em, as the secretary of your society was not present to take minutes, wouldn't it be well for me to draw up a report of this morning's pro" —

The sentence was cut short by a tremendous crash, a heavy fall, and a noise as of breaking glass and timbers above stairs.

"By Jove !" cried Theophilus, "what's that ? "

With my heart in my throat, to say nothing of the hot coffee, I flew up the stairs, followed by children, servants, and Theophilus bringing up the rear. When we reached the first landing, what a spectacle presented itself !

There, in the hall, lay a confused heap of rubbish, composed of what remained of our superb new hat-stand, splinters of rosewood, umbrellas, canes, cloaks, hats, Aggy, and any quantity of broken looking-glass.

The furniture was precious; but, of course, humanity ranked first. We pulled Aggy from the ruins.

"What *is* the matter, child? Are you killed?" I asked, almost hoping that she was.

"'Spect I be, dat's a fac," replied the girl, glaring around her in a frightened way, but moving off nimbly enough as she spoke.

"O Aggy, you naughty girl! what were you doing? How came you to break the hat-stand?" I demanded, endeavoring to restrain my temper.

"Donno; 'spect I'us too hebby fur it," answered Aggy sullenly. "'Tain't wurf nuffin'."

By dint of super-woman exertions, I succeeded in getting the rubbish cleared away, and restoring order without becoming exasperated. Theophilus provoked me dreadfully, however, by saying he wished he could stay at home, and see the fun.

Why attempt to detail the tortures of that first day? It was over at last, with all its trials and aggravations, and my weary head pressed its uneasy pillow. Children and servants were asleep, Aggy was long ago stowed away in her little room, and in the quiet of the starry December night Theophilus and I held a consultation.

His arguments were unanswerable; his sarcasms scathing; but I held my ground. A few mishaps at first, I urged, were to be expected. In a day or two the girl would improve — indeed, there was a slight change for the better already — Philly would become ashamed of his foolish terrors — it was a clear case of charity — and, in short, I wanted to give the girl a fair trial, because — because — I wanted to.

At last the energies of Theophilus, overcome either by sleepiness or the force of my reasoning, began to flag. He had even said, " Perhaps so, my dear ; " and after that, his replies grew fainter, more wavering, and, like certain rare visits, very few and far between. Finally, after waiting nearly five minutes for a reply to a perfectly self-evident proposition, I heard something.

Not from Theophilus : he had gone off on a dream-journey, like Christian, leaving his poor wife in the City of Wakefulness. It was a noise in the house !

Not a daytime noise ; but one of those stealthy, indefinable, long-interval noises, that, coming in the darkness of the early morning hours, make one's blood creep and curdle ! Creak — creak — softer and softer — then dying away entirely. Pshaw : I thought, it's the back shutter ! No : shutters don't throw up a phosphorescent light ; and now, looking from my bed into the room where the children slept, I could plainly see a faint glimmer through the ventilator window. This ventilator, or "well," went through the centre of the house, from basement to roof. In a moment the light, though faint still, grew stronger, more definite. It was the gleam of a lighted candle from below, flashing an instant, then vanishing.

"Theophilus ! " I cried, in a stage whisper : "wake up ! quick ! "

He turned over like a sick buffalo.

"O Theoph ! " bending nearer, and giving him a slight shake, "*do* get up ! *there's a man in the house !*"

" Ye-e-s," grunted my natural protector, " I know it ; go to sleep, dear."

There's no use mincing the matter. I did get agitated :

7*

I poked him, shook him, jerked the pillow from under his head, and finally restored him to consciousness.

As thoroughly alert now as myself, he sprang to the floor, and, after a few hasty tiptoe preparations, started for the basement, pistol in hand.

I rushed frantically into the children's room, and sat on the foot of their bed, inwardly praying that the robber's blood might not be upon my poor husband's soul.

Good heavens! The stealthy steps were coming up the stairs, approaching my very door!

I flew, and locked it.

"Em," said Theoph's voice outside, "if you want fun, come down."

Decidedly relieved, I hastened into the hall. He motioned me to follow him silently. Arrived at the head of the kitchen-stairs, Theophilus crammed the corner of his dressing-gown into his mouth, and made signs for me to look.

There on the lowest step, sat Aggy; a lighted candle and the open cake-box were on the floor beside her, and on her lap was a half-eaten apple-pie, which she was rapidly demolishing.

"*Aggy!*" cried Theoph, in an awful voice.

The pie fell from her lap, as, with a scream, she darted up, flew to the end of the kitchen hall, and stood at bay, with her back against the door.

"Aggy," said I, "what in the world possessed you to come down here like a thief, at this hour of the night, to take what did not belong to you?"

She crouched to the floor, looking up at us nervously. Something in the expression of our faces re-assured her.

"Couldn't he'p it nohow, missy: I was 'mos' starved. Don' lick dis nigger dis time, missy."

She had eaten three hearty meals that day, to my certain knowledge; but a chance glimpse into the dining-room pantry had proved too much for her.

"I shall not whip you, Aggy," said I, "though you have done a very wrong act. Put the cake-box back into the pantry.

She obeyed.

"Now go to bed, and never attempt any thing of this kind again. Do you hear?"

"Yes, missy. I'se sorry for 'sturbin' you, missy, I jess is," answered Aggy, bending furtively to the floor, and clapping a big piece of the broken pie into her mouth; "but I likes 'em dreffel."

Obeying a sign from Theophilus, the damsel preceded us in our ascent with perfect decorum, until half-way up the garret flight, when apparently seized with some droll idea concerning the night's adventure, she broke into a loud "Gorry!" and doubling herself with laughter, bounded with something between a spring and a caper, up to her room. In a moment or two we heard her clear voice falling through the "startled air" in an.exultant verse, each line ending with a jerk, as though the undressing process kept time with it: —

> " All de good people when dey die —
> Hally-lujee-rum !
> Go to lib in de happy sky —
> Hally-lujee-rum ! "

All things considered, it was astonishing how well our

charge comported herself for a day or two after this. My kindness-principle evidently worked well, and I was not without hope that Aggy might yet become a useful member of society. To be sure, she had some very troublesome peculiarities, such as shouting, in a loud but not unmusical voice, snatches of hymns and quaint negro songs, at all hours and under the most inopportune circumstances; snapping her great white teeth at poor Philly whenever she caught him alone, thereby throwing the little darling almost into spasms; and, when not watched, invariably going up stairs outside the balustrade, to the delight of the children, who risked their necks daily in humble imitation. Shoes and stockings were her especial detestation; and in many a delightful barefoot hour did she elude my vigilance, sometimes going, like

> " . . . my son John,
> With one stocking off and one stocking on,"

in order to have a presentable foot ready for a surprise. On these occasions, meeting her suddenly in the halls, I, dupe that I was, contented myself with a glance, little suspecting that the fact of her hopping, or being perched upon one foot, meant any thing more than an every-day antic.

Added to these eccentricities was an inconvenient habit, strangely out of keeping with her usual animation, of falling asleep any time and any where. Keyholes and cracks of doors were a certain conquering power with her. Many a time we found the creature lying at full length upon the floor, her ear pressed to the carpet, and every nerve strained to catch the conversations going on in the room below; and more than once Theophilus, entering his library, found her curled up on the rug, match in hand, sound asleep before his unlighted fire.

One of the most singular traits of the girl was her sudden fits of temporary docility. Often, at these times, I would speak to her of her good old father, and of that higher Love which knows no difference of hue or tongue. She would listen attentively, and even kneel beside me, repeating word for word some simple prayer with true pathos in her tone, only to break away at last with a contemptuous "Pooh! what stuff! Dis chile can't stan' sich truck, missy!" Or she would suddenly change to a sitting posture on the floor, and with hands clasped about her knees, rock backward and forward, wagging her head between each chuckle, "Oh! Lorry me, missy, you kill dis nig; you do. Yah! yah! it's wuss den wucken, he! he!"

But, as already stated, Aggy really did improve in many respects. She soon learned to scour the knives, build fires, and wash and scrub in a way that quite propitiated Ann and Nora; though Ellen, my fine waitress, would not be appeased. "Nagers was what a dacent girl cuddent and wuddent putt up wid, nohow." She left, and I conceived the wild idea of trying Miss Aggy as her substitute.

A few days' indefatigable drilling did wonders, and, I am proud to say, produced a profound impression upon Theophilus. To be sure, she generally ate half the sugar from the bowl while setting the supper-table; and dishes of pickles grew strangely less on their way from pantry to dining-room; yet she was generally good-tempered, and, when "massa" was absent, very anxious to please. Why *he* should have had such an influence upon her is incomprehensible; but there is no denying the fact,

that a word or a look from him always either frightened
her immoderately, or possessed her with the spirit of a
hundred imps. Now and then, especially when we had
friends to dinner, mischief reigned supreme. At such
times interference or notice only made matters worse.
The more important the guests, or the greater the solici-
tude of poor Theoph that no *faux pas* should occur, the
more apt was her ladyship to wickedly fill the tumblers so
full that they could not be lifted without accident; or to
slyly take possession of the knife and fork of some embar-
rassed guest; or even to burst into a shout of laughter, or
cut an unexpected "pigeon-wing" in the fulness of her
mood. I shall never forget the day that the Rev. Dr.
Barrilpreech dined with us. Just in the middle of his
impressive grace, Aggy burst into the room, singing at the
top of her voice,—

"I'se boun' fur de lan' ob Canaan,"

and then apologized with,—

"Gorry! missy, what yer habbin' bressin' *to-day* fur?
Missy Grimmons use ter hab 'em *reg'lar*."

After this Theophilus became unmanageable. I was
constrained to hire another waitress, reserving Aggy for
the "generally useful" department. Here her principal
labors resolved themselves into eating, drinking, sleeping,
and hiding between her mattresses every stray article in
the house. Odd shoes, pieces of old suspenders, empty
spools, bits of ribbon, tea-spoons, tooth-brushes, and even
Theoph's cigars, all were stowed away with equal care and
cunning. How they got there, Aggy never could "tink."
"Mus' hab bin de cat or Philly;" she "didn't know nuffin'
at all about 'em."

One day Theophilus remarked rather pompously to a friend at dinner, that of all the books in his collection, he valued most a certain rare edition of Sir Thomas Browne. "You shall see it to-day, sir," he added, "as I know you will appreciate it." After dinner my beloved bibliomaniac attempted to fulfil his promise. The precious volume was gone! Theophilus was in despair. He had been reading the book that very morning. At last, with an intuition quite equal to De Quincey's "electric aptitude for discovering analogies," I stole up to Aggy's room, and slyly disinterred Sir Thomas from his tomb between the mattresses. A moment afterward my unsuspecting Theophilus was surprised at finding it in his chair, "just where he had left it."

Still I repeat and insist that the girl steadily improved.

A few weeks after Aggy's advent circumstances compelled me to commit a conventional sin, — in other words, to tell a polite lie, — by announcing, at one of the sewing-meetings of our society, that I would be *pleased* to see the ladies at our house on the following Wednesday.

Now, I love freedom. I idolize soldiers. But, for all that, I do *not* like to hold a sewing-society meeting, with its scraps and threads, on our velvet carpets. Yet the thing had to be. Indeed, St. Grundy sent me a consolation by way of reward. It would certainly be a triumph to exhibit Aggy, in her advanced state, to the society. No other member had been able to keep her longer than a week. She should attend the door. I felt there could be no chance of accident in that, while, at the same time, the neat appearance and improved bearing of the girl would speak for themselves.

Wednesday arrived.　Concluding that discretion was the better part of valor, I did not betray my anxiety to the damsel, but simply directed her to remain in the hall, make no noise, and to admit the visitors respectfully.

Every thing worked charmingly.　As I stood at the end of the long rooms, engaged as "cutter," I could hear Aggy's pleasant voice saying, "In de frun' parlor, ladies ;" and now and then a cheery, "Yes, marm, I'se berry happy," in answer to some kind inquiry.　She attended to her duties so promptly !　The ladies had not time to ring the bell before they were admitted, and so noiselessly too, by my little handmaiden.　I was quite elated, and could not forbear indulging in a few remarks to those near me concerning Aggy's improvement, and the immense pains I had taken to make her a good servant.

"Yes-s ! ? " said Mrs. Winthrop, replying in a rapid scale of C ; and I translated it, " You have indeed succeeded, my dear Mrs. Brown.　How in the world did you acquire such wisdom and energy ? "

Our meeting over, the company departed almost in a body.　As soon as the last lady left the house I called, in a cheerful voice, from the parlor, —

" Come here, Aggy."

Her sable face appeared at the door, grinning with satisfaction.

"You have been a very good girl, Aggy, and shall have sponge-cake for your supper."

" Tanky, missy," was the honest response ; " but, bress yer ! dis nigger didn' take no troubl'.　I jess lef de do' stan'in open, an' hitched up on de hall table, dis way."

She vanished.　She was suiting the action to the word. With a sinking heart, I hurried into the hall.

My young lady was indeed upon the table, swinging her *naked* feet therefrom in great glee.

"Good gracious, child!" I cried, seizing her by the shoulder, "where are your shoes and stockings?"

"Gorry!" ejaculated Aggy, drawing up the offending members in a twinkling, and blinking her great eyes at me in terror.

There lay the cast-off articles, in full view, midway between the entrance and the parlor-door.

"When did you take them off?" I gasped, ready to cry with mortification, as the memory of my rather boastful words surged within me.

"I tuck 'em off 'fore de ladies cum," whined the girl, "coz yer tole me ter be quiet: can' do nuffin' in dem yar shoes."

"Aggy," I asked, in a tragic voice, "did you swing your feet in that outrageous manner while the ladies were in the hall?"

"Donno, missy," sobbed Aggy, scratching her head; "mose like I did, coz dey allers swings nat'ral when I sits on any thin' high."

Just then Theophilus came in, and, rather than put him in possession of the facts, I hastily gathered up the girl's *impedimenta*, and allowed her to depart for the kitchen without further comment. But it was trying, to say the least of it, to hear her singing obliviously, as she bounded down the stairs, —

> "Oh! I'se goin' to be an angel —
> I'se goin' to be an angel,
> An' lib in de big blue sky."

In the evening Aggy's father came in. He was a noble-

8

looking negro, though evidently worn by toil and suffering. His " Well, gal ! " and the twinkle in his bright eye as Aggy entered the room, told their own story of love and long forbearance. For his sake my resolve to return her to the society was abandoned at once. I shall never forget the glow of honest pride with which he forced upon me a small sum of money, — his first savings as a free man, — " to buy de chile some close."

" Ef it's de same to you, marm," was his dignified reply to my remonstrance, " I'd ruther de gal ud hab it. She hain't had no mudder since she woz a nussin' chile, an' ole Cudjoe's nebber had no chance to hev the 'sponsibility uv her afore. May de Lor' bress you, marm, an' de gem'man too, fur shelterin' uv her an' larnin' her." He looked at Aggy a moment, and continued, " An' oh ! missus, ef yer could, ef yer only could, wid de Lord's he'p, make her a Christian, it ud "— He stopped, and burst into tears.

" We will try," I said, grasping the old man's hand ; " and you, Aggy, I know, will endeavor to be a good girl for your father's sake."

" Can't, missy," sobbed Aggy, with sudden vehemence, as she plunged her woolly head in the old man's bosom, " 'tain't no use — I'se 'fractory — sojers sed so — I'se got de debbil in me ! "

At this point Theophilus walked into the room with the baby in his arms. Aggy sprang up in an instant.

" Dar, missy, dat's it ! *She* ain't a bit afeard uv niggers — she's liked Aggy frum de furst, 'cept Nora sed yer'd es leaf hev a monkey han'le her es me. Ef yer'd on'y let me hole an' ten' de baby, I cud be a Chrisshen — I tink I cud — dat's a fac."

And with these words, after wiping her eyes upon her apron, she commenced dancing frantically before the baby, stopping occasionally to let the soft dimpled hands clutch at her wool while the little one crowed and screamed with delight.

Half tempted to consent, and yet dreading a positive fiat from Theophilus, who idolized the baby, I turned the subject, and was glad when the door-bell summoned Aggy from the room.

After old Cudjoe left, Theophilus and I held another consultation. He was inexorable.

"What!" he cried, "let that crazy imp take care of the baby? never! Isn't it enough to have the furniture, windows, and crockery broken; to find the children's 'hooples' hung across my best beaver; to be made ridiculous before my friends; and to have my youngsters all talking and laughing like darkeys, without having poor little Pinky's brains dashed out into the bargain! I tell you, Emma, this notion of yours is Quixotic, absurd, positively criminal under the circumstances!"

Now, when Theophilus forgets himself in this manner, I simply blush for him, and quietly resolve to follow my own calmer judgment. Consequently, Aggy was duly installed the next day as under-nurse, and did so well, that before the first week elapsed even Theophilus admitted that matters were not so very discouraging after all.

One bright, icy afternoon — shall I ever forget it? — while little Philly, at the prospect of a bath, was suffering under a severe attack of Psychrophobia, the baby, held in Aggy's now careful arms, was gazing through the window panes. Suddenly, like Rasselas, she was seized with an ardent desire to visit the outer world, and, of course, soon set up a vigorous "dey-dey! dey-dey!" which, being interpreted, means, "I want somebody to put on my street fixings, and take me out — quick! quick!"

"*Do* lef me take her, missy, jes in frun' ob de house; please do, missy," pleaded Aggy, pressing the baby to her heart in eager anticipation. "I keep her wrap up jess es warm es I kin, an' I promis," she continued, rolling her great eyes solemnly till they showed more white than black, "I *promis* I wunt go no furder dan de house."

"Very well," said I, " I'll trust you, Aggy. Look up at the window every few moments, and I'll wave my hand when I wish you to come in."

We wrapped the little darling up warmly, and I couldn't help congratulating myself on my recognition of Aggy's true sphere, when I saw how tenderly and cautiously she descended the stairs with her precious burden.

In a moment I raised the window, and saw Aggy walking demurely up and down in front of the house, her head bobbing like a mandarin's in dutiful watchfulness of my signal. I could not resist the temptation to run down to the front parlor, where Theophilus, in dressing-gown and slippers, sat reading the paper, to show him how gloriously my system worked. He looked up as I entered.

"Theoph, dear, do come and see how carefully Aggy carries the baby," said I, raising the sash lightly.

Aggy was singing in a subdued voice, as she paced slowly up and down, —

> "Massa gone, missy too,
> Cry! niggers, cry!
> Tink I'll see de bressed Norf
> 'Fore the day I die."

All would have been well, if Theophilus had only kept quiet; but the man was possessed. He dashed the blinds open with a bang, and called out sternly, —

" Be careful, girl! The sidewalks are slippery. Mind you don't go a single step past the house ! "

This was enough. Aggy raised her eyes to his face, and we saw in a flash that her impish spirit was aroused. Off she started. Theophilus, without taking time to get coat or hat, rushed to the door, and reached the side-walk just in time to see her dart around the corner. He hurried on, but only to catch the gleam of the baby's white cloak, as it disappeared at the next turn. Another, and yet another corner was gained with no better success. People stared to see a hatless man rushing along at such a rate. Crowds gathered, and every idler in the street joined in the chase, but to no avail. The girl had wings to her feet. Theophilus shuddered, lest in her excitement she should dash the baby to the ground ; but he dared not slacken his pace, because to lose sight of her, he felt, was to lose his child forever. Shouts filled the air : cries of " Stop, thief ! " — " Run, sis ! " — " Shake your pins nimbler, old fellow ! " — " Hurrah for the gal ! " resounded on every side. Meanwhile the rabble, Theophilus in their midst, pressed on faster and faster. More than once the fugitive ran almost under the heads of passing horses, causing them to leap and prance ; but she never once faltered or staggered. On she ran, until, turning her head, she saw that her pursuers were gaining upon her. Halting an instant, she laid the baby on a pile of mats in front of a grocery, and flew around the corner.

No one followed ; for all stopped to see whether what

8*

she had cast away was a bundle or a living thing. Not a sound escaped it ; and only when its panting father clasped it to his bosom, did the poor frightened birdie utter a cry. Theophilus told me afterward that *that* cry was the sweetest sound he had ever heard in his life ; which struck me as rather a queer idea, though I said nothing.

Poor Theophilus! His position, considering his temperament, was certainly not an enviable one. Standing in slippers, bareheaded, with a screaming baby in his arms, nearly a mile from home, and in a part of the city where not a hack, not a hat-store, was to be seen, surrounded by a gaping crowd, who deluged him with questions, and incensed him with their jokes, he was indeed to be pitied ! Matters were not much ameliorated either by the appearance of a policeman, who coming late to the rescue, as usual, insisted in stentorian tones upon knowing "what all this meant."

Humbled and grateful, I clasped the baby in my arms that evening, scarcely daring to look at Theophilus.

We might never have heard of Aggy again, had not our little one been carried to Madison Park, months after, by its new nurse.

When they returned, I could hear baby chattering in pure Choctaw all the way up stairs.

" Why, darling, what is it ? " I asked, meeting her at the door, and almost smothering her with kisses. " What did baby see in the park ? "

"Goo goo, Ag, goo goo, Ag, zoo whoo ! "

" Bless her heart, ma'am," cried nurse, " I declare if she don't almost tell you."

"Tell me what, Betsey?"

"Why, do you believe, ma'am, when me and baby was a-going in the park, what should come bouncing up to us but an ugly little nigger?"

"Ag! Goo-ug, gug!" explained the baby.

"Yes, you pet: goo goo. So it was," continued Betsey, taking off its "things," and putting all the pins into her mouth: "it was a nassy black thing, it was."

"Well, what about the colored girl?" I asked, becoming impatient. "Was it Aggy?"

"Yes, ma'am, that very young un you've been tellin' me of. Well, if she didn't laugh and cry and dance, and clap her hands, till I thought she'd go into fits. Then she whisked the baby out of my arms in a jiffy, and most strangled it with kisses; and, do you believe, ma'am, the more I tried to pull baby away the more it wouldn't come, but just held on to the dirty black neck, and hollered. At last, when I got baby safe in my arms again, and it a-screaming to go back to her, I jest up an' told the sassy thing to go about her business.

"'Well,' says she, 'I'se gwine' (these niggers talks like heathen). 'Tell missy Aggy lub her fus-rate, on'y I'se got anudder missy now;" and ran off, after kissin' baby again, and laughin' and cryin' like wild."

Betsey paused from sheer exhaustion; for during the narrative she had been tossing her charge up and down, shaking her head, and making herself interesting to it generally.

"Ran off? Didn't you call her? Couldn't you stop her?"

"Bless you, ma'am! There ain't a person living could

'a' stopped her.   Why, she run faster than the very wind, ma'am.   I misgive me she's kind o' wild, savin' your presence ; or maybe she's afraid the master'd have her took up, — as most any gentleman would after such work. P'r'aps " —

" But didn't she say she would come and see the baby ? Didn't she tell you where she is living ? "

" Not a word, ma'am," persisted Betsey solemnly, shaking her head.   " She just run and run, as if the very terrors was after her."

That was the end of it.   Aggy, who is no creature of fancy, but a real, living girl, never again ventured near the spot that held Theophilus.   She was gone, and with her my philanthropic scheme, but not my faith in her race, my hope for their future.

Often in the quiet spring afternoons, while sitting in the nursery, that lithe figure seems before me again ; and I almost hear her quaint snatches of song ringing through the house.   When baby shouts with keener delight than usual, the clatter of those wild dances once more rings in my ears ; and often in the dim twilight, the old father's words come back : " Ef yer could, ef yer only could, wid de Lord's he'p, make her a Christian ! "

INSANITY OF CAIN.

INSANITY OF CAIN.

HATEVER is startling in the fact of questioning Cain's sanity only goes to prove the simple justice of the doubt. For more than five thousand years humankind has been content to look upon the First Born as a murderer. Each new generation, convicting him as it were without hearing of judge or jury, has felt far more concern that the conviction should be understood as a so-called religious fact, than that a remote and defenceless fellow-creature should have the benefit of human justice. One-tenth of the zeal and candor with which our own Froude has endeavored to make a saint of England's chronic widower might have sufficed to lift a world's weight of obloquy from the shoulders of Cain. But, until to-day, no philosopher has chosen to assume the difficult and delicate task. No jurisprudent has dared to investigate a charge that has been a sort of moral stronghold for ages. So grand a thing is it to be able to point away far back, deeper and deeper, into antiquity, to the very First Families, and say, Behold the fountain-head of our murder-record.

Doggerel has much to answer for. It has driven many

a monstrous wrong into the heart of its century.   It has
done its worst with Cain, but not *the* worst.

> C —— is for Cain,
> Who his brother had slain,

though winning in cadence, lacks spirit as a charge.   It is
too non-committal.   The feeble soul that contrived it was
fit only for jury-duty.   It wants the snap of preconceived
opinion.   But CAIN, THE FIRST MURDERER, is grand,
unique, statistical.   Hence its vitality and power.   Generation after generation, taught to loathe his very name, has
accepted the statement on general principles.   There had
to be a first murderer ; and why not Cain ?   Again, why
not Abel for the murderee ?

There was no miasma in that sweet, fresh time ; no
scope for contagious diseases.   There were no pastry-
shops, no distilleries, no patent medicines, no blisters, no
lancets, and no doctors.   Consequently, there was no way
for a man to die unless somebody killed him.   Cain did
this thing for Abel.   That we do not dispute ; nor that he
did it gratis and unsolicited.   But was he a murderer ?
Setting aside the possibility that Abel's time had not
come, are we to judge Cain by the face of his deed ?
May there not have been palliating conditions, temperamental causes ?   In a word, was he sane ?

For centuries, ages, the world has overlooked the tremendous considerations involved in this question, placidly
branding an unfortunate man with deepest ignominy,
and taking it for granted that his deed was deliberate, —
the act of a self-poised, calculating, and guilty mind.   Let
us see.

In the first place, Cain, for a time, was the only child on earth. That in itself was enough to disturb the strongest juvenile organism. All the petting, nursing, trotting, coddling, and watching of the whole civilized world falling upon one pair of baby shoulders! Naturally the little fellow soon considered himself a person of consequence, — all-absorbing consequence, in fact. Then came Abel, disturbing and upsetting his dearest convictions. Another self! A new somebody! A kicking counterfeit, held fondly in *his* mother's arms, riding to Banbury Cross on *his* father's foot!

A Brother? What did it mean? There were no books to tell him; and if there had been, the poor child never knew a letter. There were no philosophers nor metaphysicians in those days to explain the phenomenon. The earliest Beecher was not born; Darwin was still a lingering atom in some undreamed of, unorganized pseudo-protoplasm of a monkey. The child had no friends, not even a school-fellow. Adam's time was taken up with what modern conundrumists have called his express company; Eve had the baby to mind, and Cain was left alone to brood over the unfathomable. Think of the influence thus brought to bear upon the delicate, sensitive brain of that very select child. A mature intellect would have given way under a far less strain.

But Cain survived it. He became reconciled, we will say, to the little Abel. They played and shouted together as children do in our day, racing the fields at will, growing to be strong, brave little animals, fierce, impulsive, and aggressive — especially Cain. But how did they fare æsthetically — no academies, no Sunday-schools, no gymnasiums, nothing to direct and balance their young minds !

Their parents were plain people, caring little for society, we imagine, and any thing but dressy in their tastes. There were no lectures in those days, remember; no concerts, no Young Men's Christian Associations, to make life one long festivity — every thing was at a dead level. Probably the only excitements Adam and Eve had were thrashing the children and making them "behave." Whatever sensation Adam may have made among the beasts of the field, the only public movement possible to his active-minded wife was to notify all mankind (i.e., little Cain and Abel) to look out, for Adam was coming! Naturally, Abel, being the baby, the last and therefore the best and dearest, was spared these thrashings and public excitements to a great extent; and so the burden of social responsibility fell upon poor little Cain. Who shall blame him, or wonder at the act, if now and then he indulged in a sly kick at Abel, — Abel, the goody boy of the family, the "rest of the world," who would not on any account be as naughty and noisy as brother Cain?

Yet who of us can say that any such kick was administered? At that early stage of his existence, the controlling mind of Cain had not yet given way.

It is no light matter to be the first man in a world like this; and Cain certainly was preparing to hold that position. Adam, his father, was created for a purpose. Like Minerva, he sprang into life full grown; therefore, though we may safely consider him as the first human creature, he certainly was not the first man. For how can one be a man who never was a child?

Here we have another argument in favor of Cain. Besides having no bad boys to pattern after, he was under the constant direction of his parents, who certainly, if only from an instinct of self-preservation, would have trained him never to be passionate or cruel, when in his right mind. To be sure, they labored under a peculiar disadvantage. Herbert Spencer himself, coming into the world booted and spurred, with no childhood to look back upon, might have been at a loss how to manage the first boy. We must never forget that there was a time when instinct and reflex action had the start of the doctrine of precedent and law of consequences; when the original "I told you so!" had yet to be uttered. Even the warning example of Cain was denied to the moral advancing of this first boy.

Still the situation had its advantages. There were no fond uncles and aunts, no doting grand-parents, to spoil the child, and confound the best endeavors of Adam and Eve. Fortunately for the boy, Poor Richard's Almanac was yet unwritten; George Washington's little hatchet was never brandished before his infant mind; and Casabianca had not yet struck his attitude on the burning deck. So young Cain was spared a host of discouraging influences. In short, there is every reason to believe, that, in spite of depressing conditions and surroundings, he grew up to be at least a better man than his father, who never had any bringing up at all. That he did not kill Abel in his boyhood is proof enough of this. There was discipline somewhere.

And in the name of developed science and Christian charity, why not, in considering subsequent events, make due allowance for whatever phrenological excesses the cranium of young Cain may have possessed ? An intelligent father of to-day, figuratively speaking, can take his child's head by the forelock. He can detect what is within it, and counteract proclivities. If an ominous bump rise near his baby's ear, he is ready to check combativeness with "Mary had a Little Lamb," "Children, you should never let," and other tender ditties. In a word, he may take observations from the little mounts of character on his child's head, and so, if he be wise, direct the young life into safe and pleasant places. But Adam knew nothing of phrenology. Nor have we great reason to believe, that, if he *had* known of it, he would have discreetly followed its indications. Children are not always cherubs. We all know how the dearest of our little ones sometimes become so "aggravating" as to upset our highest philosophies. Was Adam more than human? Say, rather, he was the fountain-head and source of human passion.

Again, both children were the victims of an abiding privation. They had the natural propensities of childhood. They had teeth, stomach, appetite, — all the conditions, we will say, of cholera infantum, — except the one thing for which they secretly yearned, — green apples ! These, of course, were not to be had in that house. They were not even allowed to be mentioned in the family. Not once in all their lonely childhood were those children comforted with apples. Think of the possibilities of inherited appetite, and then conceive of the effect of these years of unnatural privation !

Again, who shall question that at times the deepest and most mysterious gloom pervaded that household? Even if Adam and Eve did not confide in their children, their oldest boy must have suspected that something was wrong. *What was it?* — the terrible something to be read, and yet not read, in the averted faces of that doomed pair? They evidently had seen better days. Where? Why? How? What had become of some vague inheritance that Cain felt was his by right? Morning, noon, and night, misty and terrible suspicions haunted his young mind. Night and noon and morning, the mystery revolved and revolved within him. Was this conducive to sanity?

Conceive of the effect of the animals seen in the children's daily walks! There were no well-ordered menagerie specimens then, with Barnum or Van Amburgh in the background as a foil against terror. Savage beasts glared and growled and roared at every turn. Whatever geologists may say to the contrary, we must insist that the antediluvian animals did not necessarily antedate Adam. Taking the mildest possible view of the case, the plesiosaurus, pterodactyl, mastodon, and megatherium, in their native state, could not have been soothing objects of contemplation to the infant mind.

Well, the boys grew up. But how bleak their young manhood! No patent-leather boots, no swallow-tails, no standing-collars, no billiards, no girls to woo, no fellows to flout! Nothing to do when the farm-work was over, and the sheep in for the night, but to look into each other's untrimmed faces with a mute "Confounded dull!" more terrible than raving.

Fathers of to-day, would your own children pass unscathed through such an existence as this? Your little Abels might stand it, but how about your little Cains?

9*

Would they not "put a head" on somebody? Would they not become, if not stark, staring mad, at least *non compos mentis?* Gentlemen of the jury, these considerations are not to be lightly passed by.

In judging of Cain, look at the situation. On the one hand, a terrible family mystery, no schools, no churches, no lectures, no society, no amusements, no apples! On the other hand, the whole burden of humanity borne for the first time; paternal discipline; undue phrenological developments; monotonous employment; antediluvian monsters; antediluvian parents, and an antediluvian good brother, in whose mouth butter would have remained intact for ages.

Undoubtedly that brother had an exasperating smile. He was happy because he was virtuous. He had a way of forgiving and forgetting that for a time would deprive the offender of reason itself; above all, he had a cool, collected manner of his own, added to a chronic desire to be an angel. His offerings always fulfilled the conditions. His fires needed only to be lighted, and the smoke was sure to ascend with a satisfied, confident curl far into the sky.

Cain's, on the contrary, refused to burn. We can see it all. The smoke struggled and flopped. It crept along the ground, and, clinging to his feet, wound about him like a serpent. It grew black and angry, shot sideways into his eyes, blinding and strangling him —

And there stood Abel beside *his* pile, radiant, satisfied, wanting to be an angel!

It was but the work of a moment. The pent-up, disorganizing influences of a life-time found vent in one wild moment of emotional insanity. Abel was no more!

Why dwell upon the tragedy? The world is familiar with its sickening details. We shall not repeat them here, nor shall we question the justice of the punishment that came to Cain, — the remorse, the desolation, the sense of being a fugitive and a vagabond on the face of the earth. He had killed his brother, and the penalty must be paid. Sane or insane, a terrible retribution must have overtaken him. But how about his guilt? Would it have been the same in either case? Are hereditary organism, temperamental excitability, emotional phrensy, to be disregarded? No! a thousand times NO! What "competent juror" would acquiesce in such a proposition?

"Am I my brother's *keeper?*" cried the poor wretch, when called upon to name the whereabouts of the missing Abel. Who can doubt here that Cain, like any lunatic of our own time, believed himself alone to be sane, and those about him stark mad? His use of the word "keeper" proves this. True, there were no lunatic asylums in that day; but if the first original representative "inmate" was at large, where should or could the first representative keeper be but in that inmate's diseased imagination?

Friends, the time has come when this case must be taken up. Its mighty issues can no longer be set aside. If Cain was not sane at the moment of killing, the stain of murder must be wiped from his brow now and forever. This tardy justice may at least be done him. Our children and our children's children must be taught to speak of Cain the man-slaughterer; Cain the mentally excitable; Cain the peculiarly circumstanced; but Cain the murderer? Never!

A man's own testimony shall neither convict nor acquit

him.   But are we not to take into account, as indicative
of his state of mind, actions and declarations coincident
with the commission of the crime alleged against him?   If,
at or about the time of the fatal deed, there was positive
evidence of incoherence, what then?   Witness the last
recorded words of Cain : —

"EVERY ONE THAT FINDETH ME SHALL SLAY ME."

Is this the utterance of a sane mind?   "*Every* one that
findeth me, shall slay me?"   Gentleman, Cain at this
point was not only crazy — he was the craziest man that
ever existed!   No ordinary lunatic, however preposterous
his terrors, expects to be killed more than once.   But to
this poor madman retribution suddenly assumed a hydra-
headed form.   His distracted brain, unconscious that
Adam was the only other man in the wide world, instantly
created an immense population.   He saw himself falling
again and again by the strokes of successive assassins,
even as Abel had fallen under his hand.   His first dazed
glimpse of death expanded and intensified into a horror
never since conceived by mind of man.   His happiness
overthrown ; his reason a wreck ; a prey to fears that
stretched before him forever, with no possible hope of
final destruction, — the only consolation is, that he could
not know the merciless verdict of posterity.   He did not
recognize in himself The First Murderer.   Rather than
dream of such ignominy as this, was it not better that he
should cry in his ravings, " Every one that findeth me
shall slay me ! "

We leave the question to the intelligence and the justice
of this faithful and enlightened century.

SHODDY.

SHODDY.

"Show me the fortunate man, and the gods I forget in a moment." — SCHILLER.

OMEWHERE on this broad earth can always be found fit prototypes of the most wildly-conceived heroes and heroines of the fairy-tales. There are little Jacks in our day, subduing giants quite as formidable as those of the time of the great Blunderbore. The genii steam and electricity are offering seven-league boots and listening-caps to old and young; and bean-stalk ladders ·are springing up at the feet of the restless Jacks whom fortune favors. The age has its drowsy Gullivers and its wide-awake Lilliputians; its Sindbads, big with adventure; and its "army of faithful believers," tilting at every thing. There are still Pussies-in-Boots, faithfully serving my lord the Marquis of Carabas; daughters spinning weary threads from distaffs never growing less; social harps which at last cry "Master!" and waken terrible ogres, and inquisitive wives vainly trying to re-polish the tell-tale key. We have Blue Beards, with sheathed cimeters, grimly extending their matrimonial relations; and sister Annies ever watchful of another's needs. There are Sleeping Beauties,

107

alas! by the thousand; and fair ones with golden locks for whom princes and poets struggle. There are beasts, too, whom we learn to love, after we have entered their rose-lit sanctuaries; and monsters who have sung, —

> "Fee! fo! fum!
> I smell the blood of an Englishman!"

There are Strong-backs who bear the world's burdens, and Hop-o'-my-Thumbs who contrive to slip its responsibilities; maidens, whose tongues shed dangerous vipers, and maidens whose words are a shower of roses and pearls. Proud sisters are every day being humbled, and patient Cinderellas dropping the slipper that shall win them the prince. Foolish old couples are wasting their "wishes" on black-pudding; and wise younger ones are finding the "treasure of life" in each other. There are saintly, ministering Red Riding-hoods, and, Heaven save the mark! grandams, with very big eyes and ears, eager to devour them. Men and women are still sighing for the waters of perpetual youth; and duenna-dragons are guarding enchanted and enchanting maidens. There are Ali Babas and envious Cassims; sham oil-merchants and avenging Morgianas; wicked but lucky peddlers and tailors, like those in the tales of the brothers Grimm; and Aladdins with very wonderful lamps indeed!

And here, after drifting down the stream of fairy lore, we cast anchor; for it is with these peddlers and tailors and Aladdins that we have to deal. In short, at the risk of mixing the metaphor, I propose to "strike oil," the oil that fills the Aladdin-lamps of our own matter-of-fact day, when men cry *Cui bono ?* to every thing, and expect title-deeds to castles in the air.[1]

The discerning reader need not be told the name of this oil ; nor that the tailors and peddlers alluded to, with their fleet-winged geese and magic packs, are the so-called Shoddy contractors of the land of Stars and Stripes.

Verily, it is true. In this fair land, the wildest tales of fairy chroniclers are rivalled by every-day experience. What are the exploits of Ali Baba compared with the discoveries of those who first said "Open Sesame" to the caves of Cali Fornia ? And what was good Mrs. Cassim's zeal compared with that of the indefatigable Want-to-get-rich of modern days ? Then, when the caves were opened, how everybody rushed in, some coming out richly-laden, and some finding themselves (metaphorically) drawn and quartered, like poor Cassim ! But why tell an old story ? There is newer material for fairy work than this. There are these tailors and peddlers and Aladdins, at whom all America is just now gazing with distended eyes, wondering at the new palaces flashing into existence, at the streams of wealth flowing into startled pockets, at the presto-touch changing ragged clowns into dazzling "gents," and, above all, at the fearful spell being cast upon American life by these strange creatures, lifted, as it were, by enchantment, into sudden wealth and importance.

We shall consider the peddlers and tailors, i.e. the shoddy contractors, first. "Shoddy," according to one Simmonds,

---

[1] This paper originally appeared in the London Cornhill Magazine, about a dozen years ago. It is given a place in this volume because it records a state of things that in some respects has passed away, and become part of the social history of the Republic.

— whom both Worcester and Webster use as a cat's-paw in handling the ugly dissyllable, — is "a fibrous material obtained by 'devilling' refuse woollen goods, old stockings, rags, &c. It differs from 'mungo,'" he says, "in being of an inferior quality, and is spun into yarn with a little fresh wool, and made into coarse cloth, drugget, padding, and other articles."

So say the lexicographers. But, in this fast age, yesterday's dictionary is almost as much out of date as yesterday's newspaper. In the world's great book of synonyms we find that shoddy has been given a far wider signification. If Liszt, in his "Life of Chopin," can devote pages to the explanation of the Polish word *zal*, we should require volumes fairly to describe the American word "shoddy." It means pretence, vulgarity, assumption, the depth of folly, and the highest height of the ridiculous ; also gilded ignorance, mock-patriotism, wire-pulling, successful knavery, swindling, nay, treason itself. On the other hand, it implies innocent good luck, reward of merit, and the miraculous and sudden appearance (in the newly-rich man) of super-intelligence and all the cardinal virtues. It means vast expectations in hovels, and discomfort in palaces ; hippoo-birds, wretched with *real* golden crowns, the secret envy of hippoos with the comfortable yellow crest common to hippoodom. It means bare penury in the father, and gorgeous affluence in the son. It *will* mean ignorant dismay in the son at the scornful superiority of the grandson, and grandsons who will feebly ignore the name and character of the founder of their illustrious house.

And this word, with its varied meanings and strong significance, has been raised to its present altitude by no less a lever than the great American Rebellion.

Now, a great rebellion calls for two things, — men to carry it on, and men to resist it ; and these, whatever may be their several patriotic aspirations, their valor, and enthusiasm, must be fed, clothed, and equipped. Their respective governments, having no time to lose, stand on the " outer wall " of circumstance, and call loudly for the vendors of food, clothing, and ammunition to draw near. Honest industry hears the call, and prepares to answer it as far as conscience and means will allow. Meantime enterprise, whether honest or not, pricks up its ears, — " Hallo ! here's luck ! country in trouble — wants something in a hurry — no time to examine — little down-hearted, I see — no harm in cheating the government." And the consequence is, a contract made so advantageously to the Treasury Department, that honest merit sighs, "I can't afford to go in," and settles down to the old routine.

The fortunate contractor at once buys up all the floating " poor stuff " at home and abroad ; and his minions, with their sub-contracts, fatten themselves like vampires on the poor sewing-women of the land. Then come immense supplies of army-clothing, — flannel under-shirts, made of " human creatures' lives," and blankets and uniforms of veritable " shoddy." The armies march forth in gallant array. Soon follow innumerable catastrophes like that described by an observing troubadour of 1861 : —

> " ' March ! ' said the colonel. ' Forward, march ! '
> Crack went the seams in halves !
> A hundred steps, a hundred men
> Showed just two hundred calves ! "

Notwithstanding this sad event, confiding officials still trust to the shoddy garments. They fade and rip, and burst apart, and drop to pieces, but the contractor feels secure. His fortune is made, let the soldiers shiver and curse as they may. What are a few thousand poorly-clad men to him? *He* is comfortable, in his marble halls.

Then come the peddlers with their packs, every thing by this time valued at an exorbitant rate; for must not the army be fed and equipped? With lying tongues and exultant hearts they present their wares. The inspectors are in a hurry; in fact, their eyes are dim with war-smoke. Every thing is "passed," — leaky tents, glued shoes, mouldy oats, hickory beef, rusty pork, poor muskets, and worse ammunition. Broken-down horses and donkeys are transmuted (on paper) into war-steeds and mules; and leaky, unseaworthy tugs, ycleped "vessels" by Shoddy, are sold at fabulous prices for the pursuit of nimble privateers, and the safe transportation of the country's defenders. The treasury grows lean; but, like Mynheer Von Dunderland, the peddler-contractors grow fat. They count their gains in hundreds and thousands and millions; they thrive and feast and are merry, while their victims, they who feel the real weight of their iniquity, are cheated of their soldier-death, and must fall in swarms, from the effects of insufficient shelter, bad food, and positive poison.

Of course there are marked exceptions to these contracts and contractors; but that they are exceptions, and not the rule, seems to be generally admitted.

When a great nation, overgrown with the mosses of peace, is stirred and shaken like a huge rock on the wayside, we all know what squirming, slimy things run forth helter-skelter ; how they wriggle and reach and burrow ; how nimble and eager and greedy they are, and how they fatten on the disturbed *débris*. But when the sunshine peers in among them, and freshening winds play about the old foundation, these slimy things soon disappear amid the chirp and hum of a better activity. This sunny-breeze state of things is now prevailing at the North ; but there are crowded graves east and west, — in the Shenandoah Valley, on the green banks of the Potomac, and the sunny slopes of Virginia, — on which the Shoddy contractors dare not look ; and homes, the very atmosphere of which should stifle them.

If there are Shoddy sinners, there are also Shoddy saints ; men who, having committed no wrong, find themselves suddenly very " well off ; " contractors, too, some of them, who fulfil their part like good Christians, and, strange to say, make money by that same. A certain class of lucky inventors, inspired speculators, sudden-rise-of-property men, and men who have " struck oil," or gambled successfully in stocks, make up the rest of the ranks of Shoddy ; and strange, motley ranks they are, swelled by the consequences and requirements of the civil war into a formidable body indeed.

Shoddy has its shibboleth, but it is difficult to detect it amid the din of the times. It is *en mascarade*, and therefore not always easily recognized. It has changes of surface like the chameleon, and stages of development rivalling the wonders of the polliwig. It can darken the very air around, and yet, like Peter Schlemihl, it has far more " substance " than shadow. Full of mysteries and contradictions, how shall we detect it ?

Shoddy minces its words with anxious affectation; Shoddy pours forth slang with a recklessness unparalleled; Shoddy carelessly jingles its wealth, and invites mankind to come and see; Shoddy clutches its gains with the sleepless vigilance of the miser. Villanous Shoddy rises to a foam of sparkling benevolence; virtuous Shoddy, like the rat in the fable, preaches industry to the starving from a pulpit of cheese. Shoddy sinners doze in the best pews on Sunday; Shoddy saints stay at home, paralyzed by their sudden good fortune; Shoddy merchants stand well " on the street;" and Shoddy merchants dodge the sheriff round the corner. In fact, there is scarcely a form of human antithesis in which this same Shoddy does not shine supreme; and we in turn bemoan it, laugh at it, despise it, envy it, insult it, and flatter it. We warn our children against its example, and sedulously emulate its display in our own humble manner. We cry, " Lord be merciful unto these miserable sinners!" even while we long to be able, in some mysterious and consecrated way, to go and do likewise. We sneer at Mrs. O'Flaggerty's huge diamond, and conceive an intense dissatisfaction concerning the "mean little stone " that once had power to gladden our hearts. In fact, I am afraid, if Shoddy be absurd, we are foolish; if Shoddy be sinful, we are without charity: but let that pass; what we have to deal with now, is the serpent itself, not the community that, " charmed " and scotching by turns, is in danger of writhing within its folds.

Nothing could be a greater mistake than to consider Shoddy as an invariable synonym for newly acquired riches. Men are frequently to be found who cast no

reproach on sudden prosperity, but rather exalt good fortune by accepting it. These can hardly be called Shoddy,
though their entire wealth come in a day. Neither, of
course, can those be so classed who, by inheritance, fall
from the bare limb of "good family" into the warm nest
of plenty; nor those whose honest gains, long withheld,
are unexpectedly rendered to them *en masse.* The lines
are wiredrawn, and yet the practical distinction to a close
observer is as broad as day.

When you see, as I have seen, a coarse-visaged, angular
woman, dressed — or rather covered — in the very extreme
of the mode, weighted with velvet, silk, and sparkling
jewels, and hear her exclaim, "Lor! expense ain't no
manner of consequence to us?" you will undoubtedly
detect a taint of Shoddy in the air. When you hear an
"honored citizen" boasting, in bad English, of his well-
known wealth and general can't-be-beativeness, you will
know that Shoddy is not far away. When you enter a
magnificent mansion, redolent of newness and fashion,
and search in vain, amid the gorgeous upholstery, showy
frescoes, and mongrel adornment, for the trailing home-
flowers of elegance and repose, be sure that " Shoddy" is
written on the wall.

Sometimes a mere glance, or tone, or footfall, will
betray the presence of Shoddy ; or a comment on life,
science, art, music, or literature, will proclaim it as from
the house-top, though you may have passed its legions,
unaware, in the street. In brief, to really comprehend
Shoddy, you must see its home, hear its conversation, and
observe its actions, note its tastes and desires and aspirations. Then, and not until then, you can say, " *This* is

Shoddy," — "*This* is *not* Shoddy," with the force of a
Delphic decision.

Meantime, this deponent, having valiantly penetrated its
recesses, can offer certain personal testimony which may be
of interest.   No matter how or why these glimpses were
obtained.   Enough to say "I have been there to see."

Never shall I forget my first *entrée* into those hallowed
precincts.   We were a party of four, two ladies and two
gentlemen, who, in consequence of having received a gold-
lettered invitation to Mrs. G——'s grand reception, had,
on the appointed evening, proceeded in state to her showy
residence on Fifth Avenue, New York, — an avenue, by
the way, believed by "the Shoddy" to lead to heaven
direct.

Our "dressing-room" experiences were peculiar, and
suggestive of strange scenes to follow; but being, as we
believed, well endowed with the repose of the Vere de
Veres, we descended toward the scene of action with a
tranquil consciousness of being in every way equal to the
occasion.   At the very foot of the stairway we were
accosted by no less personages than the hostess herself,
and her grown-up daughter.   The latter looked pale
and anxious; but the mother, gorgeous in an intensely
blue silk, and a huge coronet of pink and purple artificial
flowers, evidently felt no misgivings.   Both stared at us
unconditionally.   Suddenly a light illumined the countenance of the elder lady, as she broke forth in a loud,
emphatic tone, —

" *Well*, I declare !   Mrs. D. *and* Mr. E. !   How *do* you
do?   And Miss E. !   glad to see you, I'm *sure;* but the
lights and every thing dazzles me so, I don't hardly *know*

people. Miry, my dear, this is Mr. E. and Mrs. D., both kind friends of your pa, and Mr. E.'s daughter." (Aside to me.) "*Who* did you say the other gentleman was? Oh, yes! Mr. Stevens. Glad to see *you*, sir, you may depend. *Young* gentlemen are *so* scarce. Couldn't hardly get up the party for it. The war, you see, takes the best of 'em off. Oh, excuse me; ha, ha! I didn't mean no offence! But every young gentleman at a party counts *one;* don't they, Miry?"

"Lor', ma!" simpered Miss G., blushing violently. Here Mr. Stevens, always superbly master of himself, gracefully hastened to the rescue, and in a moment Myra was laughing the girlish laugh which, thank Heaven! even Shoddy cannot make unmusical.

"Dear me!" sighed the matron pathetically, without offering to allow us to pass into the drawing-room. "They've been pouring in thick as sirup all the evening! I'm so exhausted I can't hardly stand up."

Then followed a painful silence. Through the arched rosewood doorway we could see the gayly-dressed throng within, — a sea of blue, pink, and white, in which frantic creatures in black broadcloth and white neckties seemed to be insanely bobbing and whirling. Suddenly the music ceased. The waves, crested with gauze and gossamer, heaved violently for a moment, then parted like another Red Sea, and an army of Israelites, bearing silver trays laden with ices, passed safely through the temporary opening.

"Gracious!" exclaimed the hostess at last, with an apologetic start, "I ought to take you in. Miry," she added, nodding her head sidewise towards us as she spoke, "you must introduce them."

"O mother!" was the *sotto-voce* reply, "I can't do it: I feel too used up."

"Yes, you must," — very austerely, — "*I* sha'n't do it."

Instinctively our devoted band, feeling that this "introduction" was inevitable, glanced at each other to ascertain whether any especial peculiarity rendered us unpresentable; but we were faultless.

Myra pouted, and looked toward the animated sea aforesaid, as if contemplating a suicidal plunge.

"*Myra Jane!*" pursued the now irate mother, "do as I tell you, miss, and stop putting on airs!"

The refractory daughter was conquered. "Well, mother," she replied in a stage whisper, "I'll do it altogether, but I can't introduce 'em *separate.*"

Thus encouraged, we humbly followed the young lady; and, after being presented in a most novel and remarkable manner to the staring mermaids and mermen, we found ourselves slowly drifting toward an anchorage in the glittering saloon.

Young faces were there, radiant with intense enjoyment; older faces, with a startled, puzzled look upon them, as though the unaccustomed scene wrought more anxiety than pleasure; hard faces, varnished with a mastic smile; soft, uninterpretable faces, which were either saintly or horribly vicious; and faces without any expression at all.

Meantime the violins, being "under treatment," were relieving themselves by sundry melancholy squeaks. Groups of gentlemen, who seemed to have been recently presented with their hands and feet, were making desperate efforts to appear at ease. Neglected dames were sublime in a wretched nonchalance. Portly individuals in watch-chains were glancing uneasily at matrons, whose coiffures rivalled the Hanging Gardens of Babylon; and youths and maidens, all apparently more or less afflicted with the dance of St. Vitus, were chatting merrily together. Of these I cannot say that, —

> " Their voices, low with fashion,
> Not with feeling, softly freighted
> All the air about the windows
> With elastic laughters sweet."

In truth, — " and pity 'tis, 'tis true," — shrill tones, positive guffaws, and giggling responses, rather predominated over the murmurs suggestive of a pleasant evening at the Lady Geraldine's; and when the music floated forth once more, there was a rush, among the dancers, for " places," that would have been quite impossible in the days, —

> " When persons of fashion and taste,
> In dresses as stout as chain armor of old,
> The parties of Ranelagh graced."

Shall I describe the dancing or the dresses? No! It is enough to say of the former that I have seen nothing precisely like it elsewhere; nor can my imagination find its prototype in the revel of bacchante, faun, or fairy. It was not wholly ungraceful, nor at all unconventional. It was just Shoddy, simple, uncompromising Shoddy, as foreign in its fulness to the New York of a few years before as the dance of Eastern Houri or South Sea Islander. Of the dresses there might be much to say, were this a fashion article, or a low-tariff essay bearing upon foreign importations. As it is neither, I will simply affirm, that, with but a few exceptions, bad taste and money seemed to have vied with each other as to whose power should predominate.

We had quite lost sight of our amiable hostess, and were contemplating a dignified retreat to the dressing-rooms above, when we saw that lady bearing toward us under full sail. There were costly laces floating about her expansive shoulders, and glittering bracelets upon her roseate arms : still there was something so grotesque in her manner and appearance, that we were forced to risk the Scylla of an alarming gravity, in order not to fall into the Charybdis of an uncontrollable smile. A pang of rebuke smote me, however, when her ladyship, in a tone of genuine interest, whispered, —

"You look kind o' lonesome, Mrs. D. ; 'fraid you ain't enjoyin' yourself ? "

"Oh, yes, indeed ! " I answered, with the ardent imbecility with which persons usually perpetrate social fibs.

"Ain't you danced ? " with a look that said, "If people dare to slight you here, just let me know."

"Thank you ! I really would prefer " —

"Nonsense ! Come along ! I ain't a-going to have no wall-flowers in *this* company. I want to introduce you to a gentleman from Washington — monstrous rich ! " (she added in an intense whisper) " made a hundred and ninety-five thousand dollars in the last two months ! "

It was in vain to resist. I remember a huge Titan in dancing-master attire, — a flabby, villanous countenance,— diamonds flashing from the centre of a wall of ruffled linen, — an atmosphere heavy with pomade, — and an

avalanche of "excuse me, marms," following sundry accidents to my attire, and innumerable heartrending deser-
tions and escapades during the progress of "The Lancers."
Beyond this my impressions are vague and unsatisfactory.
In fact, there are many things connected with the occasion
that I would "willingly let die," not excepting the monstrous rich gentleman himself.

Before the evening was over, I found myself in a smaller
apartment, gorgeously furnished and rendered truly remarkable by the abominable, showily-framed paintings
which nearly covered the walls. A human quartette was
seated upon the sofa à la Kenwig, and it needed no second
look to convince me that I saw the four children of our
hostess. Feminine treble and masculine base were represented there in equal parts ; but that effect was purely a
matter of faith, as nothing in their faces betrayed that
they ever had uttered a sound.

Soon the mother appeared. "Lor'! Mrs. D., *you* here!
Well, I *had* to get out of the parlers for a *minnit*, it's *so*
suffocating there. *This* is our family setting-room. Ellen,
stick in your shoulder, miss!" (This last was a dramatic
aside directed to the sofa department). "I see you're
lookin' at the paintin's. Well, we *have got lots* of them,
that's certain. I tell Mr. G. we'll have a picture-gallery
before we know it — ha! ha! but that's nothing, for the
man's bound to have every thing that money can buy" —

(Here a radiant, satisfied ripple of expression ran across
the quartette upon the sofa).

I tried to say something ; but alas! the allusion to the
possible art-gallery had jeopardized my gravity to such an
extent that I could only cough pathetically.

11

"This 'ere big picture," pursued Mrs. G., "is a land-scape, — a land*scape* by — children! who is this land*scape* by?"

"Mr. Benson," they all answered in a breath, closing their mouths instantly like four traps.

"Yes, Mr. Benson. He's a Western man, Mrs. D., and don't charge more'n a quarter what these New York paint-ers ask. He paints pretty, though. Ain't that white fence *too* natural?" she added, letting her head drop sideways with its weight of admiration.

Alas, the fence *was* too natural, but I did not trust my-self to say so. I merely bowed, and stared vacantly at an ideal work representing, as I suspected, Cupid and Psyche, since the blue damsel depicted therein balanced a huge butterfly upon her shoulder, and her youthful companion had the inevitable wings and quiver of the mischievous God of Love.

" *That* picture," broke forth Mrs. G., standing in superb disdain beside me, "ain't *my* taste — Mr. G. bought it. It's a fancy piece you see — Cupid and — children! what did your pa say was the name of this picture?"

"Cupid and Per-*sitch!*" answered the two elder ones simultaneously.

"Oh, yes, Cupid and Per-*sitch!* But, Mrs. D., you must look at our portraits: we've had one artist for a year past doing all our family. Here's Mr. G. and me. You *may* think the yellow gloves in my picture ain't mates — any one might — but they are. The artist was bound to put one of them 'in shadder,' in spite of all *I* could say. This is Dan'el's picture (sit up straight, Dan'el, and let go your sister's sash): it's like him, all but the hair. The

naughty boy" (looking severely at Daniel) "burnt off one
side of his curls last week, and we had to cut off the rest.
Here's our youngest, Tommy — the end one on the sofa
there — most beautiful boy! Always just as sassy and
lively as you see him in the picture: *ain't* it like him,
Mrs. D.?" And, following the example of Lord Chatham,
on a certain well-known occasion, Mrs. G. "paused for a
reply."

Shade of Polonius, pity me! Tommy was a blue, moist-
skinned little fellow, who looked as if he were in a state
of chronic somnambulism. What could I do but falter,
"Very like," without venturing to take a second look at
the original?

"Mr. Benson said he never seen a harder child to
paint," resumed Mrs. G.: "it was so difficult to get his
expression." (Alack! I should think it would have been
very difficult.) "He took him at first with only one shoe
on, and the other layin' on the carpet; but I wasn't goin'
to have a child of mine lookin' like that, so I made Mr.
Benson just change the shoe on the carpet to something
else, and put good pumps on the poor child. It's bad
enough to have your young ones looking like wild about the
house, without having their likeness took all in a muss!"

At this moment I saw, with a mingled feeling of mirth
and apprehension, Mr. Stevens and Miss E. enter the
"setting-room." The lady continued her picture-showing:
"This next one is Katy," she said: "the child ain't
as plump and rosy as that, I know, but her pa and me
felt so in hopes she'd pick up that we had her took fat.
Now, I had Ellen, here" (halting before a remarkably
pigeon-breasted specimen of high art), "painted correct in

every thing but her chest.   I ordered Mr. Benson to make
that high, because the poor child is so awful flat, that it
would only worry her father and me to see it hangin' before us all the time.   Besides, Ellen's going to Dr. Lewis's
what-you-call-it?   Children! what's the name of Dr. Lewis's
place ? "

"Gym-naz-jum!" replied the sofa promptly.

"Ah, yes! gym-naz-jum, that's it.   Well, she's going
there reg'lar after this, and Dr. Lewis says it'll soon fetch
her chest out perfect."

Oh! the agony, to me, of this protracted interview —
the consciousness of being watched by that unpitying, fun-
loving pair — the convulsive laughter deep in my very
heart as my good-natured chaperon led me from one mas-
terpiece of artistic abomination to another!   There were
a few other persons in the apartment, all speaking at once,
their voices mingling strangely with the rise and fall of
the music surging through the mansion ; but I dared not
look upon them as the irrepressible mother talked on.

"Here is something now that you *must* see" (pointing
to an execrably painted waterfall, resembling a combination of green calves'-foot jelly and gingerbread).   "*This*
picture is my daughter Miry's work ; ain't it beautiful ?
but do you know, her *real* talent is *figger-paintin'* — that's
her talent!   I showed Mr. Benson (the one that does all
our pictures, except the frames — *they* come from Goupil's)
— I showed him *this* picture, and told him that Miry's
teacher said she had great talent for painting ; and says
he, 'Madam, if your daughter *has* a talent for art, it *must*
be for figger-paintin', — he told me just from looking at
that waterfall!" she added triumphantly.

It is possible that by this time my expression had become idiotic, or at least blank. Mrs. G. evidently felt that further elucidation was required.

" Figger-paintin'," she continued, raising her voice to a didactic pitch, " is paintin' of figgers and animals, you know ; that's what the artists call it — figger-paintin' " — laying down the information with a patronizing emphasis.

" Ah ! " I ventured.

" Yes, Mr. Benson, being a painter, could put his finger right on Miry's talent — ' it *must* be, madam,' says he, ' it must be it's ' — heavens ! Ellen Ann ! catch Dan'el ! "

This startling peroration was caused by an eccentric movement of the child Daniel, who, having fallen asleep, upright, upon the sofa, was announcing, by a preliminary pantomime, his intention of shortly precipitating himself upon the floor. Fortunately, Ellen Ann was equal to the emergency. " Dan'el's " precious nose was saved, and the youth restored to partial wakefulness by means of a brisk maternal shaking.

" Gracious ! " exclaimed Mrs. G., becoming suddenly conscious that, though art may be " long, time is fleeting," " I ought to be in the parlor with the company. What *will* folks think of me ? Dear me ! what a bother ! " So saying, the lady vanished in a glimmer of blue, purple, and pink.

Those last significant words were echoed in my brain again and again that night, during the wakeful hours that followed my introduction into " Shoddy " society. Poor Mrs. G. ! what will folks think of her ? What a bother ! what a bother !

A full and faithful record of the manners and customs

of Shoddy — of its histories, thoughts, feelings, and deeds — who could write it? We have had time to afford but a glance into the home of one of the lucky "peddlers." As for the "tailors," with their fleet-winged geese, "we could, an' if we would," tell much of them — but mean time the genii of the lamp are waiting. We must move onward. Come with me to the chief domain of the great magician, he who fills the thousand lamps which Aladdins uncounted are now rubbing in bewildered delight. You will be surprised to learn what a noisy, dirty, crazy-looking place it is.[1] The good old Quaker who named the State which encloses it would lift his hands in horror at the sight. Squalid and tumble-down, yet at the same time a very wilderness of newness, with its swarming population, with its sheds, hovels, improvised hotels, and unsightly new houses, it appears to have been conjured by the magician during a severe fit of nightmare. For miles and miles, crowds of derricks rear their heads in every direction. Engines, bound to the spot, are puffing and laboring; engines on distant rail-tracks, screeching beneath an invisible lash as they hurry away with their burdens ; and huge blackened reservoirs are pouring forth torrents of wealth. Near by are the bluffs, sitting like Memnons guarding the rivers of oil beneath. Big with the secrets of ages, they lean forward as if humanity had at last awakened their interest. Sometimes a great tongue of flame darting upward, as if to lap coolness from the clouds, tells us that an oil-spring has been accidentally set on fire. Miles of carts, groaning like living things,

---

[1] Oil Creek, Venango Co., Penn.

wriggle their way through the heavy mud, led on by patient horses and swearing men. Women in motley attire, anxious to buy impossible wares, run out to meet the occasional dray of the itinerant grocer or market-man. Dirty boys, with the flutter of possible wealth in their rags, bully the scions of "recent arrivals," or anxiously hang around "dad" as he sinks the great shaft "on shares" with McConnaky. Truly "Oil Creek" presents a strange scene, and all its wildness and oddity culminate in its metropolis. Desolate and crowded, neglected and thriving, abject and enterprising, ruinous in aspect, yet grand with invisible golden domes, is Oil City; and above and around floats the breath of the great magician, stifling and nauseous to unconverted mortals, yet like a glorious incense to the pilgrims who bow down and worship him.

Verily the city is worthy of its name. Every thing is oil. The one long, crooked, bottomless street glistens black with mud and oil. The shanties and houses are oily. Oily derricks stand in the back-yards; and men with their thousands "in bank" walk the oily planked sidewalk in garments grimy with oil. Oil-boats, laden with oil, float sleekly past on the oil-covered river. Even the dogs and horses are oily; and the little fish crowding under the oily shore, find themselves packed like sardines before they know it. There are oily shops, where the very wrapping-paper breaks out in transparent blotches; and oily banks, attended by oily cashiers, where oily money is deposited as the product of oil. There is oil in the very atmosphere you breathe, oil in the water you drink, and a mysterious unction about your daily fare. The inhabitants "talk oil," too, until your senses are in danger of slipping

away from you.   Then, again, oil is the one great social
leveller.   Good "blood" is at a discount, and a derrick
can lift to the plane of the highest.   Your teamster
yesterday may be your Rothschild to-day; and your
neighbor, however detestably vulgar in speech and manner,
can snub you with a successful "drill."   If he has "struck
oil," and you have not, local ethics will exalt him, and
defy you to prove your superiority.

Here are the headquarters of the great magician.   Of
course, like other magicians, he has been for ages popping
up in all sorts of places; but it was at Oil Creek that
he first touched the rock for the benefit of modern Aladdins.   They were rough, homespun fellows, ignorant and
wretchedly poor, for their lands had barely yielded a sub-
sistence.   One would have thought them just the men to
venture desperately into the jewelled cave.   But no:
"ready cash" was too tempting.   Nearly every man of
them sold his lamp to the highest bidder, and left for
more fertile fields.   Consequently the genii of wealth and
enterprise were soon, as all the world knows, serving new
masters.

One of these Aladdins, however, had an adopted
mother, a shrewd old soul, whom we will call the widow
McGannon — catch her selling the lamp!   No, she rubbed
it, and rubbed it, and daily the genii brought her, first
gold, then "greenbacks;" she stowed the treasure away
in every nook and cranny of her tumble-down shanty,
until it could hide no more.   This was all very well.   But
one day the old lady was trying to light her fire: the
rusty stove had been troublesome of late, harboring spite
it seemed to the green wood cast aside in loading rafts

for Pittsburg. This day there was a great spluttering
and hissing when the wood went in, but no blaze. In her
dilemma the old lady poured from a bucket some of the
great magician's oil upon it, when presto! the demons of
flame sprang forth! In vain the Widow McGannon
screamed and struggled : they never let go their wreathing hold upon her until she and her money were parted
forever!

This old lady had recently drawn a will, making her
adopted son Tommy sole heir. For fifteen years past, the
young gentleman had been content to do odd jobs in the
village, diverting himself in the meantime with toad-
sticking and "making of little mud-pies:" now he collected the treasure so carefully hidden behind board,
rafter, and beam, and proceeded to investigate his affairs.

Half of the original farm had been sold by the widow
at the commencement of the oil-fever. The remainder
she had prudently divided, and leased, on shares, to different "companies," with the agreement that she should receive half of the oil obtained. By this time the yield was
prodigious. The ragged, ignorant country boy became at
once a millionnaire, with an additional income variously
estimated to be from three to six thousand dollars a day!

Remembering Malvolio cross-gartered, we need not
wonder that the widow McGannon's heir should feel
inclined to make, in Shoddy phrase, a "splurge" on the
occasion of his sudden good fortune. Young men do not
fall every day into fields yellow with real golden buttercups. Besides, Tommy was good-hearted and generous;
and, since the roots were sure to bloom again, he scattered
the buttercups in every direction.

As may be supposed, Thomas lost no time in "seeing
the world." Wherever he went, tales of his queer ways
and startling expenditure split the ears of the groundlings.
To hire the grandest suite of apartments of the leading
hotels, as he passed along ; to entertain his acquaintances,
intimate and casual, with princely munificence while he
staid, and when he left for an absence of a month or
more, to retain the rooms, with directions that his
"friends" arriving in the mean time should be "made
comfortable" at his expense. All this was a mere baga-
telle to him. There were rumors that, when he pat-
ronized the theatres (eschewing private boxes as "too
confinin'") he secured a dozen seats, in order to have
room to "spread himself," as he said ; but I record this
eccentricity with mental reservation.

Certain it is, however, that once, while visiting a Western city, he directed his friends to obtain for him "a
prime bang turn-out," which, translated, means a carriage
and two or more steeds to draw it. Soon he became sole
proprietor of a "five-thousand-dollar team," with equipage
to correspond. *Now* Tom was glorious ! Never rode
young man more incessantly. His "team" seemed destined to solve the problem of perpetual motion ; and the
gaping bystanders could hardly tell whether they were
witnessing a pleasure-ride or a "runaway."

But what youth of spirit could be expected to derive
satisfaction forever, even from a "turn-out"? At the
expiration of a fortnight, Tommy's coachman, having
vainly waited two days for orders from "the boss," presented himself before his employer.

Our Aladdin was lounging in an elegant apartment,

moodily nibbling a cigar. Perhaps he had grown tired of "fun ; " or it may be, he was thinking of a kind voice that the flame-demons had stilled. At all events, he was meditative.

The man coughed, and said, " Yer honor," twice, before Tommy looked up, with a gruff " Hey? What do you want *now ?* Who are you ? "

"John, sir, — the coachman, sir. Did you want the carriage brought round to-day, sir ? "

" No : I'm going off in half an hour, — going East."

" Goin', sir ! An' will I be stoppin' wid you any longer, sir ? "

" No, I s'pose not. Here, take this. That'll square us."

" Thank'ee, sir. Sure, that's good pay, sir. But, if I may make so bold, what's to be done wid the horses, sir ? Is it kept at Williams's they'll be, yer honor ? "

" The hosses ! Oh, I don't want 'em no longer ! I'm going off for good in a few minnits." And Tommy, quietly puffing his cigar, consulted an enormous gold watch.

"But, yer honor " —

" Oh ! go long with you. I don't *want* the team, I tell you. Take 'em, and keep 'em : kill 'em, or do what you please with 'em ; only clear out."

" Be the Lord, sir ! And is it *kape* the craytures *meself* you're sayin' ? "

Tommy nodded, gave another puff, and pointed to the door. " Yes : take 'em, carriage and all, and go about your business."

One day, when Tommy was "doing" New York, he

strode into Tiffany's magnificent jewelry establishment on Broadway, and startled the assembled salesmen with a loud, " Show us a dimond ! "

" Here is one, sir," responded an elegantly modulated voice from the " diamond department." " Eighty dollars, sir."

" Pooh ! not such a speck as that ! Something bigger ! "

" Allow me to show you this. Very pure stone, sir, — one hundred and sixty dollars."

" Nonsense — bigger ! "

Herewith the gentlemanly salesman (whom I have always suspected to be a noble lord in difficulties) produced a brilliant of about the size of a small pea. " Exquisite stone, sir — first water — eight hundred."

" Look here ! " cried Tommy, becoming exasperated. " If you've got a reg'lar dimond, fetch it out : if you haven't, just say so."

My lord, half-amused, half-vexed, here, by way of totally annihilating his rough customer, brought out the Koh-i-noor of the place. " Will *this* suit you, sir ? Moderately fine stone : price, fifteen thousand dollars."

" *Now* you're comin' to it ! " cried Tommy, decidedly mollified. " Is this the tiptop biggest ? "

" It *is*, sir," replied his lordship coolly (stroking his beard at the same time, as if to say, " Now, my rustic friend, I have wasted quite enough time upon you : you may go.")

" You ain't got nothin' bigger now ? "

" Nothing, I assure you."

" Then I'll take it."

My lord, I grieve to say, lost his presence of mind, and

stared; but Thomas at once produced a huge roll of "greenbacks," counted out the money, and the sale was concluded.[1]

This, as I am told, occurred in the early days of Shoddy. Now my lord, having become familiar with its ways and means, would scarcely lift his eyelids, were his coal-heaver to propose to buy out the entire concern.

Not all the newly rich, however, allow their money to be seen among men. There are instances in the oil-country, as it is called, of persons who a few months ago were at least tranquil in their poverty, and are now suffering all the tortures of the miser. I know of one whose wealth has come upon him so fast as literally to overwhelm him. He is bowed with the mere weight of possession. The flowing wells upon his single acre are yielding him four thousand dollars daily, as his share of the profits. He is afraid to trust to the banks, and government bonds do not look enough like money to satisfy him. He must have gold. Consequently, as fast as his money pours in he converts it into specie, and packs it in boxes and butter-firkins. These he buries in his cellar, each one, as he hides it away, leaving a corresponding weight of care in his weary heart. Nothing is added to his personal comforts, and matters of luxury are unthought of. His sole extra outlay is to hire a guard of twenty men, to watch his house night and day. A less number might suffice, but perhaps half of them are required to act as a check upon the others. Poor rich man! Who would dream his dreams, or share his waking cares, to be worth a million?

On the other hand, I can point out a late hard-working

1 These accounts of Tommy, and others, are cited from actual life.

rustic, whom wealth has truly blest. A grand, startled, honest look beams from the man's face. A millionnaire, he can hardly write his own name ; but when the first great wave of "riches" surged through his heart, some noble thoughts, long buried under the sands of want and toil, were laid bare, — thoughts that he will cherish reverently. They will tell him new things of humanity, of his own undeveloped powers. They will guide him with an unerring wisdom in training his sons and daughters. The satirists of Shoddy must bow to that man, and let him pass.

In contrast to the bright, contented spirits, bubbling up on the surface of Oil Creek prosperity, we have circulating thunder-gusts in the form of men who have invested largely in untried lands, and failed to realize their expectations. Forsaken wells are seen in every direction, their derrick-monuments marking the spot where hope and cash lie buried, without a chance of resurrection. Not more black are the smoke-stacks, everywhere dotting the scene, than the looks of these men ; and their talk is a marvellous mixture of gall and oil. Sometimes you meet a weary, well-dressed man, anxiously scanning the "operations," and asking questions of every clown and laborer he meets. He is an investigator, and he lacks "grit." You can see it in his eye. If he have not already lost his money "in oil," he will lose it soon.

One of these heavy-hearted men lately hastening along the plank sidewalk of Oil City, accidentally knocked over a starved-looking little girl, whose tattered garments seemed to have passed beyond the reach of soap.

"Oh, I beg your pardon ! Are you hurt, my poor child ? " he exclaimed, stooping to lift her.

"Go 'long!" cried the girl, springing to her feet, and shaking down her rags with immense *hauteur.* "I *ain't* poor! Dad struck ile yesterday!"

We can imagine the wistful gaze that followed the child on her onward way.

It is instructive to watch the developments of the would-be Shoddy. In the conflict of pride and cupidity, the best part of the man is taken captive, literally falling into the hands of the enemy. Instructive, too, and sad, to note the trials and mortifications befalling the elect of Shoddy. Think of the chagrin of the new billionnaire at Washington, when he saw in the morning papers comments like this on his first grand ball: "A truly magnificent affair; cost, it is estimated, $100,000, which represents the exact profit on one hundred cannon, large numbers of which have been furnished the government by this contractor."

Think of the weariness of the Shoddy lady, who, ennuied with her superb house and uncongenial surroundings, said to a friend of mine, "Ah! it's all very fine; but my old friends kind o' stay 'way from me, and my new ones make fun of me, I know they do. Every thing that money can buy I've got by the bushel; but I ain't happy, Miss Mary, I really ain't happy."

Study Shoddy while you may. It is a transient "institution" at best. Soon its strong characteristics will be lost, its peculiarities worn away. Its like has never been on earth. Remembering those ten remarkable years when speculation ran mad over Europe, when the South Sea bubble encompassed all England, and John Law ruled France with his Midas-promise and dissolving views, it is safe to assert that the Shoddy of to-day stands without a

parallel in human history.   It is the one new thing under
the sun not dreamed of by Solomon.   America, in common
with all Christendom, regards it with mingled feelings of
disgust, amusement, and concern.   " Where will it end ? "
is the question on every lip.

Verily it will end just where it began, — in human
nature itself.   It is not more American, after all, than it is
Adamite.   That it has, for the present, found a local habi-
tation and a name in America, is because nowhere else
has Nature so lavishly and unexpectedly poured forth her
treasures among the people, or a national emergency arisen
offering temptations so unparalleled, both to enterprise
and cupidity.   And Shoddy has its mission.   It will enable mankind to see more plainly than ever before the
absurdity of pretence, the vulgarity of display, and the
folly of imagining that money alone can make a gentleman.
It will point a brazen finger, for all time, at imposture and
treason, and the rottenness of the virtue that presents its
fair side to individual men, but yields to temptation in
dealing with governments and corporations.   It will de-
velop new necessities and new industries, bring a fresh,
hardy element to society, by educating new classes, open
a channel through which the poor may receive a share of
the refining influences which surround the rich ; and, what
is of very great importance, it will put money into the
national purse.

Large capitalists are needed in these days for vast
enterprises ; and Shoddy, with its bursting coffers, can
furnish its quota of these.   The Americo-Russian telegraph has its prospective message to Shoddy.   The Pacific
Railroad is its humble servant.   Other proposed public

improvements beckon to it invitingly. Science, even, is pointing the way that Shoddy must go. From north, south, east, west,— wherever gold, oil, quicksilver, or coal lie buried, — there is a call for Shoddy to come and grow richer still ; and Shoddy will eagerly answer the summons. Just now, when the nation is coming out of its struggle for life or death, when it requires fresh explorers and new resources to enable it to meet the tremendous demands made upon it, Providence reveals these long-kept secrets, discloses these hidden stores, these illimitable reservoirs of wealth, and — let us believe it — gives us Shoddy.

It may seem whimsical to begin my argument with fairy-land, and end it with Providence ; but does not life itself so open and close ? The magic delights of our childhood become recognized as God-given in our age. Our early wishes are for fairy benefits ; our later prayers are for divine blessings.

12*

SKETCHES.

MY MYSTERIOUS ENEMY.

[The following narrative is a true record of incidents which occurred in New York, not many years ago. The affair made some talk in private circles, but I believe it never got into the papers. For obvious reasons fictitious names are used. The account is given to the public in the belief that it may throw light upon the mysterious question of Natural Antipathies.]

NEVER liked him. Nay, my whole nature recoiled in terror when my glance first met his small, piercing eyes, as he suddenly passed through the reception-parlor, where I sat chatting with Lieutenant Charles. The lieutenant noticed my terrified start, and the change of color which doubtless accompanied it; for he sprang up instantly, and would have followed the intruder had I not promptly checked him, and, with a forced smile, endeavored to resume the conversation so unpleasantly interrupted.

"And you will not give me the picture, Fanny?" asked the lieutenant, after a few moments' pleading concerning my *carte de visite* which had lately been taken. "You will not give it to me!" he echoed sadly, after reading his answer in my countenance; "but surely I may see it?"

"Certainly," I answered, half regretting the coquetry

which had prompted me to deny him in the matter. " It is in my room : I will bring it to you in an instant."

Rising from my seat as I spoke, I hastened into the hall. Good gracious ! there He stood, at the very foot of the stairway, motionless, as though he had been listening to our conversation. I sprang back into the room with a beating heart, and tears of vexation in my eyes.

" You have seen him again ! " exclaimed the lieutenant, starting from his seat.

But before the door was reached my hand was upon his arm —

" No," I urged, " do not go : it will be useless, and excite an unnecessary alarm in the household. In a moment he will go away, and I will then get you the picture, and laugh at my folly at the same time."

" Your folly in getting me the picture ? " bantered the lieutenant gayly. Then he added quickly, with a new anxiety on his face, " Forgive me, Fanny, this matter is more serious with you than I at all imagined. Surely there is " —

" Say no more about it," I interrupted, trying to smile. " There are some influences which it is useless to attempt to explain. We can only recognize, and, if need be, struggle to resist them. I am ashamed of the weakness which you have witnessed this morning, and must trust to your generosity not to interpret it too harshly."

He pressed my hand respectfully, and was silent. But what meant that shrewd, almost sarcastic smile, when a moment afterward, as we heard the hall door shut heavily, he said, " Your enemy is probably out of the way now : will you bring me the picture ? "

This "enemy," as, alas! the lieutenant had only too truly called him, was, like myself, a lodger in a boarding-house. The landlady, Mrs. Hone, heard me sympathetically when, in confidence, I hinted at the annoyance he caused me, and, in her peculiar phraseology, promised "to rid the house of him" as soon as she possibly could; but begged me not to speak of the matter in the mean time, for there was nothing, she said, which she dreaded so much as "a stir" among her boarders; and among her lady boarders she was sure "this business would make a stir if any thing could."

I promised to remain silent, though more than once afterward I was tempted to regret my hasty acquiescence. Mr. Williams, a strong young man, with whom I was a favorite, lived on the fourth floor; and he could doubtless soon have effected the removal I so much longed for. As for leaving, myself, that was impossible. I was an orphan, — a dependent on a wealthy invalid uncle, who, being once comfortably settled in Mrs. Hone's excellently kept house, would not of course be tempted to leave it except for some more potent and tangible reason than I could offer.

Whether my tormentor knew my sentiments toward him or not, I cannot say; but I never, during the uneasy days that followed, heard him hurrying along the hall, or stealthily passing my room close to its very door, but I felt an involuntary shudder, and with difficulty suppressed the cry that rose to my lips. Once I met him on the stairway, and, scarce conscious of what I was doing, I bounded past him with a quick scream, and rushed into my room. *Why*, I cannot tell, except that my whole being loathed the creature, and felt a presentiment of coming evil from his presence. Not one word had we ever exchanged, and I do believe if he had spoken to me I should have fainted with terror; but his restless, intense glance had more than once met mine, and that was enough. There was a natural antipathy between us : we were born to be enemies.

Meantime my brave lieutenant had gone back to the war. He had, after all, taken my picture with him and my heart also. Only those who love, and are doomed for a while to be parted, with chances of danger and death between them, can know of the eagerness with which I awaited his first letter. Soon it came, one glorious summer afternoon, with its more glorious news : "Our army is moving rapidly. We shall fight! We shall conquer!" the letter said, "and some of us must fall; but, living or dying, dearest, remember that one heart shall" —

I read no more; for at the bare thought of the possibility of losing my hero, the half-read sheet fell from my hands, and there, in the solitude of my room, I leaned upon the window-sill, and wept long and bitterly. I loved my country, freedom, and the right; but oh! did I love them enough for the chance of this? My brave, noble lover! If he should perish, what would freedom, kindred, the light of heaven itself, be to me? Suddenly a rustling outside of my slightly-opened door aroused me; and recalled to my letter, I stooped to pick it up. *It was gone!*

Bewildered and alarmed, I hastily shook the folds of my dress, and searched floor, table, and chair, quite certain that no other human being had been in the room since I had entered with the letter, when the door opened wider, and our landlady's head, decked in all the pride of her gorgeous dinner-cap, was thrust into the apartment. Her face was paler than usual, and her manner somewhat flurried, as she laughingly exclaimed, —

"Miss Fanny, if you leave your love-letters lying about the halls, you can't expect to keep your secrets long. Not that I have learned them," she added quickly; "but some less trusty personage might have picked it up, you know."

"Mrs. Hone," I gasped, scarcely heeding her words as I almost snatched the precious sheet from her hands, "I entreat you to tell me how you came in possession of this letter."

"Why, I've told you already," she replied rather sharply. "I picked it up in the entry, just outside of your door. It was no ghost dropped it there either (so you needn't turn so white), but only that R" —

A sudden thought seemed to check her intended confidence; for she muttered something about people being so "awful nervous," and, breaking into a disagreeable laugh, hastily left the room. A moment afterward I heard her angry voice chiding Betty, the housemaid, for some real or fancied neglect of duty, with the sharp reprimand not to "leave that door open again, if she valued her place."

That door! Could she mean my door? And was I, as far as practicable, to be kept shut up in my room, so that *he* might wander unrestrainedly about the house? And what had meant my landlady's flurried manner, her sudden reticence, if in some way my tormentor had not been concerned in this mysterious occurrence? For though I by this time knew well enough *who* had taken the letter, *how* it had been accomplished without my knowledge was

13

a mystery.   It was not more than a week since I had first
spoken to Mrs. Hone of the object of my fears; and
already she would flush angrily if I even alluded to the
conversation and to her solemn promise to relieve me of his
odious presence.   She had even gone so far as to say that
"some persons were too fidgety for comfort; and for her
part, she couldn't for the life of her see what there was to
make such a fuss about.   Goodness knew, she didn't want
any such creature as him in her house; and if I thought
she did, I was mistaken: that was all!"   After this singular change of feeling, I kept my own counsel in the
matter, though I fully resolved to avail myself of the first
opportunity of persuading my uncle to change his board-
ing-place.

This was the way that matters stood on the day that
my letter was so mysteriously borne away almost from my
very hands.   After recovering it, I eagerly read it through
again and again, shuddering, in spite of myself, at a certain passage which the reader shall see.   The lieutenant,
considerate in all things, had evidently tried to express
himself so as to annoy me as slightly as possible; but it
thrilled me for all that.   Here is the passage :—

" By the way, my dear Fanny, you must know that there came into our
tent last night what seemed to me the very identical being who so startled you
that evening.   Has he disappeared from No. 123?   If so, it was himself.
If not, it was his *double*.   Size, style, and gait were the same.   He had the
identical quick, glancing eye, sharp, white teeth, and pointed nose.   Can
there be *two* such beings?   Was it from sympathy with you that I felt such
an instinctive aversion to him?   I made a dash at the fellow ; but he escaped
into the darkness as mysteriously as he had come.   Our captain and a few of
our boys were in the tent at the time, and seemed to be much astonished at my
violent movements ; and at my remarking (as I quietly sat down among them

again), 'That fellow came precious near receiving his finishing-touch,' they all protested that *they had seen no one enter the tent*, and begged for an explanation; but I chose to let them remain in their mystified condition. A mysterious coincidence, at least, was it not?"

To me it would have been a terrible circumstance; and so I told him in my reply. But my brave hero knew not the meaning of fear.

At last, after reading the letter over (I am ashamed to tell how many times), I sought the bedside of my uncle, and endeavored to render the long summer afternoon less tedious to the dear sufferer. He was aged; and the natural infirmities of his years had been hastened and increased by a slow, incurable disease. How my heart went forth toward him as, with loving hand, I brushed back the silver locks from his temples, longing that my touch might heal as well as soothe! Ere long he passed into a tranquil slumber; and carefully adjusting the sashes so that the soft breeze might play refreshingly about him, I slipped noiselessly into my chamber.

And now, at this point, I must become minute, and perhaps even tedious in detail; for I have a strange story to tell, and wish faithfully to relate the occurrences of that night.

There was but one other boarder on the second floor of Mrs. Hone's house besides my uncle and myself. This was a stern, unsociable man, named Foster; a bachelor, who always returned one's cordial " Good-morning " with an unmoved face and a jerky bow, as though his good angel had suddenly pulled some invisible string to prevent him from seeming the surly fellow he really was. This gruff personage stalked up the stairs, and into his room,

soon after I had entered mine. Our apartments were at
the back of the house, and adjoining ; though his, being
but a small chamber at the end of the hall, had its door
standing at a right angle with my own. I could hear him
moving briskly around his room for a while ; and finally,
as I arose to close my door, saw him emerge, carpet-bag
in hand, and disappear at the turn of the stairway. Soon
after there were other footsteps in his chamber, apparently
those of *two* persons ; and I could hear my landlady's
voice saying, in her usual indiscreet over-tone, —

"There is no other way : we will have to try poison,
though I dread the consequences."

Then there was some muttered reply ; and a discussion
ensued, through which I could plainly distinguish the
words, "No one in here to-night"—"never knew it to
fail"—"children"—"horrible!"—"the uncle's room"
—"danger"—"uncle can't get out of bed"—"no, it's
better here," &c.

Just then uncle's hand-bell tingled its familiar summons, and I hastened to his bedside.

"Fanny," he said, "can't you make it a little lighter
here ? I've had one of my ugly dreams; and I want to
be certain you're all right."

"To be sure I am, uncle, dear," I rejoined cheerfully,
at the same time lighting the gas near the head of his bed.
"Is that too bright for you?"

"No, no : leave it up — so. Now come tell me what
you have been doing this afternoon."

Should I tell him every thing? No. He either would
be distressed at his own powerlessness, or would laugh at
my nervous fears. So I replied, at the same time placing

a small table near his bed, preparatory to bringing up his supper, —

"Doing, uncle? Why, I have been here with you most of the afternoon; and before that I was reading a letter from " —

"Ah, I understand! Well, it's all my own fault for ever letting that fellow with the buttons have a word to say to you. I shall have to hire some fat old nurse in a year or two, while you'll be sporting around with that scamp, — hey?"

My only answer to this was a laughing threat to go to the young scamp at once, if uncle were not more respectful; though at heart I felt quite resolved, that, married or single, I should never resign my self-imposed duty of nursing him.

"Well, well," said uncle, "you've always been such a good girl I sha'n't be hard on you. See if it's time for my mixture."

"No, not for an hour yet. You must take your supper first."

"Very well. Don't put any butter on the toast to-night; and if the chicken's as tough as it was yesterday, bring up something else."

"Yes, uncle."

On my way from the dining-room with uncle's supper, I could not resist the temptation of taking a look into Mr. Foster's apartment. Resting my tray in a vacant niche at the head of the stairs, I turned the knob; but the door would not open. It was locked, and the key had been taken away. Thrust partly under my own closed door, was a pencilled note from one of the lady-boarders, re-

13*

questing, that, if my patient were well enough, I would pass the evening in her room. Well pleased at the prospect of a cheerful gossip with Mrs. Gray's delightful family, I resolved to avail myself of the invitation after my uncle had fallen into his usual slumber, and so I lost no time in attending to my evening duties.

It was nearly half-past eight before I found myself in Mrs. Gray's parlor; and by this time the beautiful afternoon had passed into a chilly, unpleasant evening. But we soon forgot outside darkness in the brightness and comfort within.

I lingered in Mrs. Gray's apartment until ten o'clock. Then, after seeing that uncle was comfortably settled for the night, I sought my own room, and, carefully locking the door leading into the hall, began to undress. This done, I stood in my long night-wrapper near the gaslight, and began reading once more the words of my absent soldier. I had just come to the passage, " By the way, my dear Fanny," when a sudden but continuous clicking startled me. It might have been the sharp dropping of rain on the roof of the piazza beneath my opened window, or the ticking of the queer clock in Mr. Foster's room; or it might have been caused by some leakage in the Croton pipes, or the creaking of the poor sick baby's cradle in the room above. It might, in short, have arisen from any of these or twenty other innocent causes; and so I tried to believe. Hastily putting the letter away, I turned the gas entirely off (unintentionally, for that matter, but my hand was not steady), and sought my pillow, quite sure that I should not sleep a wink that night. But youth and health are often proof against more serious alarms than mine had been; and I soon sank into a profound slumber.

Hours afterward I awoke with a start from some troubled dream. What it had been, I could not precisely recall; but I was agitated, and my brow and neck seemed fairly dripping with moisture. In an instant the deep tones of a neighboring church-clock striking "two" reassured me, with its familiar, every-day sound; and I soon floated off again into the land of dreams. This time the sleep was far less sound; and more than once, without quite awaking, I instinctively drew my muslin nightsleeve across my forehead. It was strangely wet, though I could feel the cool night air stealing through the darkness from the open window opposite. After turning uneasily upon my pillow for a while, I finally sank into a deeper slumber once more, and must have remained unconscious for nearly an hour, when suddenly I started up with a sense of acute pain, and, wide awake in an instant, became conscious that *I was not alone.* Else why that heavy thump upon the floor, and the quick rush that followed? All was dark; but I could feel that the pillow, my face, neck, and the shoulder and sleeves of my nightdress, were soaked with the strange, clammy moisture. Seized with a horrid suspicion, and darting from the bed in an agony of terror, I flew to the other side of the chamber, and, groping for my uncle's door, burst with a cry into his room.

Dimly lighted as it was, I could see every object distinctly as I entered; and first of all, because the long mirror hung directly opposite the door, and the small gas-jet threw its rays full upon me, I saw my own reflection in its bright surface. Great heavens! I was covered with blood! My hands were wet with it, while my cheek and throat were crimson with the streams which flowed profusely from my temples. What could I do? My uncle still slept soundly, under the effects of an opiate which his physicians had prescribed for him. Frantic with fear, I tore into the hall, flew up stairs, and would have gone into Mrs. Gray's room, had I not come into collision with my landlady at the landing-place.

"Goodness! Miss Fanny, was it you that screamed? What has happened? Hush!" — and she drew me quickly into her little room. "Why your shoulder's all wet! Gracious! child, what *is* the matter? Here, you're safe enough now: don't cry. Oh! where *are* the matches? I haven't had my room dark at night before, I don't know when. Here they are! Hush! you'll scare Mrs. Gray."

By this time the room was lighted, and apparently Mrs. Hone was as much alarmed as myself when she saw my condition. She was, however, a woman of strong nerve, and in a moment was coolly bathing my face and neck, and endeavoring to stanch the blood still flowing from my temples. When the bleeding ceased, she lost no time in changing my garments, and making me as comfortable as possible.

For some time I staid in the landlady's room, and we talked over the affair together. There was but one solution of the matter; and when, with a shudder, I suggested it to her, she answered softly, —

"Just so, Miss Fanny: it was nothing else, depend upon it. Poor child! Did you *see* him!"

"No," I whispered, "the room was dark; but I heard

him distinctly. Oh! Mrs. Hone, I can never sleep in that room again. I must leave the house to-morrow."

"Dear, dear!" exclaimed Mrs. Hone. "It's always some trouble with me, — first one thing, and then another. But I'm sure I can't blame you, Miss Fanny; though, if you would stay, I could get somebody here to-morrow who told me he could soon put a stop to all such troubles. But I hated to have him come before, because I knew it would make so much talk in the house, and make the help saucy. Goodness knows, they're unbearable enough already!"

I felt sorry for the landlady, but in my own mind fully resolved to leave her roof as soon as possible. The clock boomed "four."

"Oh, Mrs. Hone!" I exclaimed, struck with a new fear, "I have left uncle all this time. What if — Oh, will you go down stairs with me? I can't go alone!"

The landlady was naturally unwilling to run any further risk of disturbing the household, and tried to persuade me not to go, but I was resolute.

The dear old man lay there safely enough when we entered his room; but his sleep was heavy, — too heavy, and his brow was burning hot. The next day he was worse; and when I asked the physician concerning him, the reply was, —

"Oh! it's nothing very serious. Perfect quiet for a week or two, and careful nursing, are all that will be necessary."

So there, of course, was an end for the present of my plan to leave the house. But I did not attempt to sleep in my apartment again, or even to undress at all. For four nights I staid in the sick-chamber, resting only in a large armchair, or perhaps indulging in a brief repose upon the lounge. On the fifth day uncle was so much better, that, unconscious of all that had happened, he insisted upon my retiring to my own room and seeking rest. Willing to relieve his anxiety, and being really very much exhausted from continued watching, I obeyed ; and in a few moments was comfortably reclining on a sofa which stood near the window across the corner of my room.

That pleasant sunny room ! How different its appearance was now from what it had been less than a week ago ! Then all was order and neatness ; and the mantle, toilet-table, and walls had been decked with various tasteful articles and engravings, brackets and images. Now the walls were bare, and the pictures stood on the floor, ready to be taken away as soon as uncle should be able to leave the house (for I felt confident I could persuade him to go), and the little knick-knacks and souvenirs were already stowed away in trunks. The curtains were drawn tastelessly back by Betty's ruthless hand ; and on the furniture lingered a peculiar bloom, — neither cleanliness nor dirt, — left by the housemaid's duster. To add to the air of discomfort, in one corner stood a pile of trunks (which had been noiselessly packed while uncle slept) ; and in another, lay portions of a dismembered bedstead and a quantity of bedding, which the landlady had asked permission to leave there, " being as the room wasn't used."

All these things were duly noted as I lay there, vainly courting the sleep which I so much needed. I could hear my uncle's heavy breathing in the next room, and the occasional passing of footsteps along the hall, as the boarders came straggling up from dinner. It was no feverish dream then that possessed me, when there, in the broad daylight, I saw the detested creature who had attacked me in the dead of night, and the traces of whose diabolical work were still upon my temple, cautiously enter my room, and gliding slowly and stealthily along, close up to the very wainscot, actually secrete himself under the bedding in the corner !

Goaded to desperation, I leaped from the couch, and, scarce conscious of what I was doing, flew to the spot, and seizing a small bedpost which lay there, beat with all my might upon the place where I believed his head and breast to be ! No sound escaped him, but from the first stroke I felt that he was in my power. Blow after blow fell ; for I had the strength of a maniac, and I *dared* not stop. By this time my cries were heard, and the landlady and several of the boarders rushed into the room. They forced me into a seat, and lifted the bedding from the floor. There he lay, motionless ; they turned him over : he was dead — stone dead — and by my hand !

" By Jove ! " exclaimed Mr. Williams, the strong young man from the fourth story, as he lifted my victim from the floor, " he is dead, big as he is. How did you ever find courage to kill him ? "

" I'm sure I hardly know," I gasped, " except that I was desperate. He has tormented me almost to death for two or three weeks past, and last Saturday night he actually did come near killing me in earnest."

" How ? how ? " cried everybody but the landlady, crowding more closely.

The good lady winked prodigiously at me just then, and tried to change the subject; but I was too excited to heed her. Turning with a shudder from the lifeless cause of my past miseries, I explained how I had felt a natural antipathy to him from the first moment I had encountered him in the hall at Mrs. Hone's; how terrified I had been when I saw him pass through the reception-parlor where I sat conversing with a gentleman; how I had heard and seen him several times since; how he actually had dragged a letter from my room out into the hall; and, above all, how he had bitten my temple on that fearful night. I had just raised the hair carefully from my brow to show my audience the still unhealed traces of those cruel teeth, when Biddy, the chamber-maid, came bustling in. The moment she saw the lifeless body she shrieked,—

"Who killed him? Not you, Miss Fanny! I'd have been skeered to death. I'm glad he's dead, any how. I told you, ma'am," she added, turning to Mrs. Hone, "twa'n't no use tryin' to pizen him. We couldn't have had no peace or comfort after it. Then all his relations would be comin' to the funeral; and "—

"Hold your tongue!" exclaimed Mrs. Hone angrily.

Thus tenderly admonished, Biddy subsided, only murmuring under her breath, that — "Massy on us! — people's lives hadn't been safe with a critter like that runnin' round;" and finally uttering a piercing shriek as the strong young man lifted IT from the floor.

At that moment Mrs. Hone's son, Fred, burst into the room. He stopped for a moment, surveying the strange tableau. There was I, flushed with the excitement of my exploit; Biddy, angry at being checked in her voluble exclamations, and shrinking from the corpse ; Mrs. Hone, severe in her dignity as head of the house, glad that the dreadful creature was destroyed, yet anxious to prevent any talk among her boarders ; and Mr. Williams holding up the dead body so that all could see it.

Master Fred, who, being six years my junior, was my sworn admirer, and hated my mysterious foe as much as I did, took in the whole affair at a glance.

"You've killed him, Miss Fanny, have you?" he exclaimed. "Bully for you! He's the biggest fellow I ever saw! 'A rat, dead for a ducat, dead!'" he added, imitating as nearly as he could the tone and attitude of Edwin Booth, whom he had seen the evening before in Hamlet, pointing at the dead body of the huge rat whom I had just killed, which Mr. Williams was handing to the shrinking Biddy to be duly disposed of.

Possibly the reader of this narrative may, like my Lord Hamlet, have taken this slaughtered rat for "his better." If so, he has read with his imagination instead of his eyes: "a bad habit ; I pray you avoid it."

I have only to add here, that "My Mysterious Enemy" was the first and the last of his kind that ever succeeded in penetrating into the immaculate mansion of Mrs. Hone.

14

WHAT A LITTLE SONG
CAN DO.

A TRUE INCIDENT.

GAY young visitor said to me the other day:
"M——, do you remember that little English girl,
who made dresses for me last summer?"

"Yes," I replied: "she usually worked by the corner
window of your sitting-room; a delicate, fair-haired girl,
wasn't she? seemed to be a rapid sewer, — what of her?"

"Why, I heard her story lately, a terrible story; and do
you know, it seems so strange to think that during all
those days, when she used to sit and sew for me, I never
once thought of her as an individual?"

"What *do* you mean?"

"I mean just what I say. She never appeared to me
in the light of an individual. She was just the dressmaker; and whenever I thought of her, it was only in
connection with fashions and mantua-making. I remember noticing, sometimes, that the sunshine fell brightly
upon her head as she sat sewing, and that she had a shy,
trembling way with her. But it never occurred to me that
she had interests apart from her work, — personal affairs

you know, such as you and I have. It's awful to say it, but it's really true: I don't believe it ever crossed my mind that she cared for any thing but making dresses. And oh! such a terrible life as that poor girl endured! She's dead now; and I'm glad of it, poor thing. Good-by!"

"Wait a moment, Lu!" I cried: "what a strange child you are! You surely will not go without telling me more?"

"Yes, I must. It's time for my music-lesson. Good-by, dear: I'll come again soon;" and off she ran, lightly humming a tune as she hastened down the stairway.

I have not seen her since, or I should, perhaps, be able to tell you the poor sewing-girl's story. But I can relate an incident that came vividly to my mind, even before the sound of Lu's light, receding footsteps had died away.

One lovely day, in the spring of 187–, I made a startling discovery. Just when the fields were putting on their brightest green, and the fruit-trees were wreathing themselves with blossoms, I suddenly became aware that I needed raiment. All my last year's stock seemed shabby in contrast with the vernal freshness of things. In short, as my friend Helen Fitz tenderly hinted, there was nothing left me but either to look like a fright or to get some new dresses.

Then arose a new trouble: the mantua-makers were in the height of their busy season. Not one could I find who would take in another order. What was I to do? The Flora McFlimsy within me grew faint. If I should make the dress myself, it wouldn't have a particle of *style*. So my best friends assured me, with a mysterious shudder which made me feel only too thankful that my humble aspiration had been nipped in the bud.

(All this time Nature was laughing with her blossoms, and slipping so softly and easily into her new spring dress!)

Well, the only plan open to me was to employ a visiting mantua-maker. After what seemed, at the time, an endless succession of vexations and disappointments, I succeeded in hearing of that *rara avis*, — a dressmaker who not only could but would make a dress, — a visiting dressmaker, and a "perfect treasure" as Helen declared, such a "good hand at conjuring," could "fit" admirably: her only fault was that she was slow. If I could stand *that*, Mrs. Bond was the very person I wanted; and, wonderful to relate, she had a few disengaged days. So I sent a messenger, and received word in return that she would be with me early on Monday morning.

Was I satisfied then? Not quite. A strange unrest came over me; an unrest that increased as the interval of waiting diminished.

To make this thing clear, I must confess that I am of a peculiar temperament. Employees of all kinds hold a mysterious power over me. I shrink from my waiter-girl, and feel condemned in the presence of my cook. Sometimes I am almost tempted to say, " Excuse me, Ann; forgive me, Kitty. It's not entirely *my* fault that some must work while others play. I know you are far more clever at washing windows, ironing, and cooking than I should be. I never, in the world, could 'wait' at table, or answer the door-bell as patiently and cheerfully as you. I'm afraid I shouldn't have the fortitude to rise before daylight, on snowy winter mornings, and attend early mass before commencing a hard day's work. I'm not sure that

I could deny myself as you do, in order to send money across the water to bring my cousins over. In short, Ann and Kitty, if life seems hard to you, if my kitchen is dreary, and my visitors too many, forgive me, bear with me. You might, either of you, have been a poor, helpless lady yourself, you know."

The same feeling comes when with those who, higher in the social scale, still serve me; for all mankind are, after all, servants in some sense. I always submit my pulse deprecatingly to my physician, fearful lest my case be too unimportant for so august a personage; wonder what I *should* do if I had to consult a lawyer; and in church I sometimes feel so crestfallen and ashamed, that, if the sexton were not so very like the Lord Chamberlain in suppressed greatness and noiseless sublimity, I would, during the service, ask him to step up to the pulpit, and tell Dr. Blast, that, if my particular case of sinfulness aggravated him, I would willingly get up and go home.

Even shopmen are formidable creatures in my eyes. When at Stewart's, I never can throw off the impression that the clerk who is waiting upon me owns the entire establishment. But all this is nothing to the appalling influence of fashionable milliners and dressmakers. Only the thought of the lilies of the field can sustain me when in their presence.

What wonder, then, that I dreaded this particular Monday? It came, all the same, however; and when, just before breakfast, the door-bell rang, Ann, who answered the summons, was a grander, lighter-hearted young woman than her mistress, who stood in an upper room bracing herself to meet the coming presence.

14*

In a moment Ann came up, saying mysteriously, " She's down-stairs, mum, and she's had her breakfast. My! but she's the quare-looking old crayture, though ! "

" Show her up, Ann."

She entered, — a quiet-looking, mild old woman of seventy !

I had not expected this. Fancy had conjured a dressy, fussy young person, with a manner as quick and snipping as her scissors, and a roll of fashion-plates in her hand, — somebody with an iron will, who knew the exact size that a lady's waist ought to be, lungs or no lungs.

But this quiet, sober old body, clad in dingy black, how *could* I ask her to make up my finery ?

" Good-morning. Is this Mrs. Bond ? " I asked, half hoping that it was not.

" I believe it is," she answered, with a pleasant smile, taking off her shawl and bonnet as she spoke, and adjusting her spectacles carefully, so as not to tear her simple white cap. " Shall I sit here, ma'am ? "

" Oh, yes, certainly ! " and somehow, before I knew it, the old lady was cutting out a lining, and I was up-stairs again (after having taken a hasty breakfast), and seated near her, running up the breadths of a skirt, every thing just as easy and natural as possible.

Yes, she *was* slow ; but I think it was because she took so much interest in her work that she rather lingered over it. It was wonderful to see how she would turn a refractory bit of goods this way and that, until at last it would fit in exactly where it was needed ; wonderful to see her stitch, stitch, in such a steady, resolute way, and all the time with that placid expression on her face, her wrinkled little mouth pursed up, and her gray eyebrows arching mildly over her spectacles.

About eleven o'clock in the forenoon, without looking up from her work, she said, " Mrs. D——, would it be asking too much if I wanted a cup of tea at lunch-time ? It keeps me awake for the afternoon, and I can do better justice to the work."

Awake for the afternoon ! Poor old soul !

" Certainly ! not at all ! " I exclaimed, in a startled way. "We always have tea at luncheon ; but, whether or not, you should have it and welcome. Why not lie down a while, though ? Please do. Rest yourself, now, on that lounge."

" Oh ! no, no, indeed ! thank you ! " and she laughed, a quiet, sober little laugh, with a tear in it. " The tea'll keep me up now, ma'am," she added cheerily : " if you'll please get ready to try on, I'll be through in a minute."

She staid with me for three days, working steadily and slowly all the time, kept awake by the tea, and resolutely resisting my entreaties that she should take an occasional nap. One peculiarity puzzled me. On several occasions, when, after a brief absence, I entered the room, I saw her quietly slip something into a little covered basket, which sat on the floor beside her, and resume her work as I approached. Otherwise, she sewed as steadily as though she were moved by slow machinery.

But if Ann and Kitty awoke apologetic emotions within me, how much more this patient, silver-haired old lady. I could scarcely bear to see her working for me ; and it was only by planning various trifling benefits for her that I could feel in any way reconciled to it. She was so old, poor soul! and yet she so firmly thrust away the infirmities of age, as if saying constantly to herself, "That's right—back, keep straight; eyes, keep strong; fingers, keep nimble, for I have this dress to make."

Ah! if trouble were to come upon her, I thought, a real, heart-rending sorrow, she could not be like this. For it so happened that I had one great trial to bear, and I knew what important allies were youth and strength. But I did not understand her yet.

On the third day — I hardly can say how it came about — she told me the story of her life, or rather it seemed to slip from her as the work slipped through her fingers; and what a life it was! Trial upon trial, sorrow upon sorrow; prosperity at first, then misfortune and poverty; then sixteen years of married life, and three or four little graves; sickness; the prop of the home smitten down, a helpless invalid; then widowhood, with four children to support and educate; next, one of the children a hopeless cripple — labor, ceaseless labor; then sorrow and trouble in a married daughter's misfortune; then her two daughters widowed and in delicate health, and with several young children, all upon her hands, she their only help and refuge! Her youngest, an only son, she had bravely educated through it all. He had finally joined the Union army, without a word of opposition from her. At that very moment he might be lying wounded on the battlefield, or his bones might be gathered in some nameless grave, for she had not heard from him for months. And there had I been consulting with her about my sleeves!

"And you support them all, — children and grandchildren?" I asked, making believe to search for a spool of cotton, for I felt too fidgety to sew.

"Yes, deary, mostly" (she had given me this name on the second day). "Annie's laid up with her side most of the time ; and what with grieving, and taking charge of the little ones while I'm off workin', poor Esther don't earn much, though she's a fur-maker by trade. Now, ma'am, I'm ready for this shoulder again."

(How blithely she spoke ! I had been rather low-spirited of late, — I with my one illumined sorrow, she with her load of crowding cares)! As soon as the shoulder was arranged, I went into the entry to speak with Kitty concerning dinner. When I re-opened the door I saw that mysterious movement again. My dressmaker was slipping something into her basket.

"Oh !" she said, with a slight jump, "what a little thing starts me ! I was just reading my little song."

"Your little song ? "

"Yes : it's a bit of writing I've had four or five years, the greatest comfort of my life ; almost," and she lowered her voice, "like my Bible. It kept me up when I do believe nothing else would."

She said this in such a cheery way, while picking out the basting-threads, that I hardly knew how to reply. But at last I said, stupidly enough, —

"Don't you ever get sick, Mrs. Bond ? "

"No, not often ; leastwise, not enough to make me lose my day. Thank you, deary, I'll go on with that sleeve if you hain't finished it, and you can take up the cording."

"It's wonderful," I said, tacitly following her direction, "really wonderful, to think of your supporting all your family so, and on two dollars a day."

"Sometimes I *do* wonder," she said quietly, "how I do

it ; but God helps us, and then, you know, I have my little
song. I'll take them black hooks, please."

We sat silently working for a few moments. At last I
said, softly and reverently, —

" Mrs. Bond, will you teach me your little song?"

She looked up with a surprised — " What, deary ? "

" That little song you were speaking of. It would do
me good, too, I am sure. Will you teach it to me ? "

" *You*, child ! You don't need it, — young, bright, and
happy. It's only for tired old bodies like me."

" Ah ! but perhaps I do," I persisted : " life is very vex-
ing to me sometimes."

She bent down, and, lifting her little basket, slowly
raised the lid, then took out a folded piece of paper, worn
and dingy. She opened it tenderly as she handed it to
me.

" This is my little song, deary. I know all it says ; but
it always helps me to read it, especially when things comes
into my mind that oughtn't too."

I had expected to find one of the sweet old hymns that
tell of comfort and joy to come, as a reward for sorrow
suffered here. But the verses that I saw surprised me.

" Where did you find this poem ? " I asked.

" I didn't find it. The Lord sent it to me sort of mysterious. A young girl read it out once in a room where I
was sewing; and when I had a chance, I asked her to write
it down for me. I don't take to such things, gen'rally ;
but this song is kind o' by itself."

And so it was. For the poem was Adelaide Procter's
" One by One."

" I have a whole book of verses written by the same

lady," I said, still looking at the paper : "shall I bring it, and read you a few of them ? "

" No, deary, I thank you kindly; but most like I wouldn't understand 'em. This little song'll last me out well enough. As you're looking at it, deary, would you mind saying it for me out loud ? "

For the first time during our conversation, she laid down her work, and leaned back in her chair, while I read in a voice that tried not to tremble : —

" One by one the sands are flowing,
    One by one the moments fall ;
    Some are coming, some are going,
    Do not strive to grasp them all.

" One by one thy duties wait thee,
    Let thy whole strength go to each ;
    Let no future dreams elate thee,
    Learn thou first what these can teach.

" One by one (bright gifts from heaven),
    Joys are sent thee here below ;
    Take them readily when given,
    Ready, too, to let them go.

" One by one thy griefs shall meet thee,
    Do not fear an armèd band ;
    One will fade as others greet thee,
    Shadows passing through the land.

" Do not look at life's long sorrow ;
    See how small each moment's pain ;
    God will help thee for to-morrow,
    So each day begin again.

" Every hour that fleets so slowly
    Has its task to do or bear ;
    Luminous the crown and holy,
    If thou set each gem with care.

" Do not linger with regretting,
    Or for passing hours despond ;
Nor, the daily toil forgetting,
    Look too eagerly beyond.

" Hours are golden links, God's token,
    Reaching heaven ; but one by one
Take them, lest the chain be broken
    Ere the pilgrimage be done.''

I looked up.   Mrs. Bond was busily sewing, her "whole
strength" going to the present duty, her little wrinkled
mouth pursed intently as usual, her gray eyebrows arched
mildly above her spectacles, and her sweet old face more
placid than ever.

Adelaide Procter is with the angels now.   The tumult
of this busy world shall never more disturb her.   But she
is a gladder, more blessed angel, we may be sure, whenever that dear old woman reads her little song.

The Spirit of the Water-
FALL.

A HUSBAND'S STORY.

LLA M'FLIMSEY was cousin to the world-renowned Flora, but she was a better girl. Fair, stylish, coquettish, with bewitching blue eyes, and hair of the fashionable golden hue, she was the pride and glory of our set. I had gazed upon her, given her smile for smile, and more ; had attended her through scores of " Germans," and gone to paradise with her on the wings of the Redowa. Her very fans and gloves were daguerrotyped on my soul. Yet, looking back, I cannot remember that I had ever heard her seriously give an opinion, or utter even a sentiment to reveal of what manner of woman she was. As for her daily life, all that could be known to me was that she flourished in the " best circles," and in every way comported herself as became an unmurmuring child of fashion. I, a busy bee all day and a butterfly at evening, found my flower under the gaslight ; and, under the gaslight I hovered about her, enchanted, yet not quite satisfied. Some ruthless spell

seemed to hang over her beauty. Face and form were
perfect. Her hair, too, ah, how lovely it was! and yet,
even in its sunny meshes the demon of — shall I say it? —
of ugliness seemed to lurk. "Sunny meshes" hardly
describes it — ah, sunny maze! Yes, a sunny maze over
her temples; and beyond that —? But it was beautiful
hair — *that* I said to myself a hundred times. What,
then, was the mystery? Something within me recoiled
even while I admired most ardently; and she, poor child!
seeing my waywardness, wondered (I knew it in spite of
her well-trained, beautiful eyes) — wondered and grew
serious — between dances.

Alas! we knew not the direful spell that had been cast
upon us! But the end came at last. Now that all is
over, I am vexed that I did not in some way take trouble
by the forelock, and grapple with it single-handed. But I
have said I wooed as a butterfly flits about a flower.
Do butterflies think? When an ugly blight threatens a
peerless blossom, what can her Papilio do but hover
wretchedly overhead?

One stormy December night (she has told me all about
it since) my poor Ella, returning from a brilliant "reception," sought her chamber puzzled and unhappy. Almost
in tears, she flung jewel after jewel upon her dressing-
table, jerked the drooping flowers from her hair, and
loosed the glittering zone, which, it had seemed to me,
was all that kept the gauzy clouds trailing about her from
floating away into the air. Then came more arduous
toilet undoings; there were curls — two long, golden,
beautiful curls — then braids — then a golden mass of
wealth, and then the maze! But why speak of these. She

was sad — she, my matchless flower, my pearl! Ah! if I could have seen her then, seen her *earnest*, but an instant, perhaps — but no. The spell was not yet broken.

It had been a brilliant evening. Even Cousin Flora had pronounced the affair "faultless." The Harrises, the Van Doodles, everybody in town, — that is, everybody worth knowing, — had been present; and Ella had stood acknowledged belle of the hour. But it had been the same, or nearly the same, every night for weeks and weeks. She was weary. It may be her soul was asking "Is it well?" I had been hovering near her, as usual, fascinated, yet secretly dissatisfied; and she, in some strange way, had felt slighted and distressed, though she must have known that at least a dozen among those who looked upon her were longing to cast their fate and fortune at her feet. Ah! it is a cruel problem this of life. It should know better than to force itself upon a gay, sinless girl. With a sigh, Ella, after dimming the gaslight, put on a long, soft robe of wadded cashmere, and cast herself in a big armchair by the fire. Dear little blossom! Did the great senseless thing know what it held, I wonder?

How plainly I can see her sitting there, in the flickering firelight, with that new sadness on her face. The lofty room, with its curtains, its frescoed panels, its carvings of dull, dark wood, its dainty work-stand rarely used, its costly rack of books never opened, its delicate traceries of gold, its soft, harmonious colors, its toilet-table (a marvel of lace with rosy draperies blushing through), — all these were quite familiar to me; for the apartment had sometimes done duty as "the gentlemen's dressing-room," and afterward that very armchair became — But I must not anticipate.

How long Ella's reverie continued she cannot remember. It was broken at last by a sharp sense of dread. Her eyes had been fixed upon the toilet-table. Fascinated by its cloud-like canopy and curtain, where pink and white seemed floating together in airy softness, with here and there a bright gleam from the fire deepening its hue, she had wondered whether the effect might not be something like the "early dawn" that travellers talk about, — when suddenly its curtain was stirred!

What could it mean? There was not space enough under there for a robber to stow himself. Her pet spaniel she knew was already sound asleep in the housekeeper's room. Cats and kittens were forbidden the house; but it might possibly be that some vagrant puss had stolen in during the day.

Even this solution almost paralyzed her with fear. After all, it might be merely fancy.

With a half-smile at her weakness, she sat upright, and looked steadily at the offending drapery. It stirred again — not feebly this time; but with a quick, resolute movement — stirred and parted !

A bouncing little figure stepped forth.

"Blaze up, Fire !" said the little figure, "and let the lady see me."

Instantly the fire sent out frisky jets of flame.

"That's right," said the figure jauntily. "Now, am I not a beauty ? "

A beauty? It was the ugliest of all ugly gnomes, goblins, or whatever one might choose to call it. It was short, stumpy, of a dingy brown, and *made entirely of matted hair !* Even its arms were of the same material;

and its eyes were formed of rings of white and black hair, with the light of a golden curl shining through them.

"Who are you?" gasped my poor girl, ready to faint.

"Who am I?" pertly replied the figure: "why, one of your friends to be sure. My name is Sheniona. I'm the Spirit of the Waterfall!"

"Oh, oh! Go away!" shrieked Ella.

"All in good time, my dear," said the visitor coaxingly; "all in good time. Now, *don't* be frightened in that foolish way. I'm sure I expected a different reception from *you*. But never mind that. Business is business, you know. If I hadn't had business I would have staid away — though, really, who would have dreamed that you could hate me so, seeing *that*" — and Sheniona nodded significantly toward the toilet-table.

Ella was gradually becoming less alarmed: there was a saucy, friendly air about the Spirit, that was rather winning after all; so she ventured to ask timidly, —

"What business?"

"Well, my dear, business of rather an embarrassing nature, if you *must* know. (Brighten up, Fire!) The fact is, though I seem such a plucky, self-reliant Spirit, I am really somewhat dependent upon others. In short, if it were not for others, I couldn't be the beauty that I often am. (Now, Fire, don't be lazy!) I'm Queen of them all, and they know it. Every one bows to the Spirit of the Waterfall. But you see, my dear, sometimes those who have been forced unconsciously to help me get to be a little troublesome: they come again and again, pestering me and asking for 'their own,' as they call it. Even when I haven't used 'em a bit they keep whining out, 'It's all

15*

your fault — all your fault!' till I'm most dead. It's enough to put me all out of tangle — it really is;" and the Spirit struck a despondent attitude.

"Well?" asked Ella, longing to make a rush for the door, and yet not daring to stir, "what's all this to me?"

The Spirit laughed a quick, fuzzy little laugh.

"What's it to you? Well, if that isn't *too* much! Why, it's every thing to you (Fire, don't go to sleep, please) — every thing to you just now, I mean. The fact is, you've got something that don't belong to you, and the owners want it.

"I?" faltered Ella, "I?"

"Yes, you," answered Sheniona, with an encouraging nod. "Now, don't be so nervous. Brush up; do! I've no idea of calling you a thief. Neither have they. Of course you haven't intended to do any thing wrong. But they want 'their own.' They've been at me ever so long about it ; and at last I thought I'd just lay the matter before you. What do you say?"

"What do I say? Oh, yes! take it, good Sheniona, whatever it is, and go home."

"Home!" echoed Sheniona scornfully, but in a smothered tone, "what do I want of a home? *My* object is to make headway in the world ; but that's nothing here nor there. Besides *I* can't take it. They must help themselves. What do you say, — yes, or no?"

"Oh, dear! y-yes," answered Ella, closing her eyes.

"Very well. That's something like. Now, good people, you may come. Fire!"

This last ejaculation was not a military order to the "good people," but was addressed in a warning "aside" to the members from Liverpool. Accordingly the room grew light in a twinkling.

Ella tried to keep her eyes shut, but they opened in spite of her. In every corner of the apartment she saw women ; not exactly ghostly women, — though they could not have been mortal, since neither door nor window had opened to admit them, — but women very different from those whom she was in the habit of seeing ; and every one of them was looking reproachfully at her.

"Now," commanded Sheniona, in an injured tone, at the same time collecting something from the toilet-table, and throwing it into Ella's lap, " now come and claim your own."

Ella trembled. As the women slowly approached, she noticed that they made no sound as they walked, and that the heads of nearly all of them were closely cropped. They gathered in silent groups about her, casting eager glances upon what she held on her lap. She tried to rise, and throw the coveted things upon the floor ; but she was powerless.

Suddenly one of the women, a worn, dark-browed crea-ture, came close to her, and, bending, snatched one of the articles. It was a curl (yes, one of the very curls that I had seen drooping upon Ella's bosom that evening !).

" This is mine ! " she cried fiercely.

" Yours ! " sneered Sheniona, " what did you ever do with that, you old raven ? "

" I'll tell you what I did with it. I held it to my heart a thousand times with the only thing I loved on earth. I kissed it night and day. I stroked it on my poor, toil-stiffened fingers until some of its gold seemed to light up my soul. It was like a chain leading me to heaven. But harder times came. I couldn't get any work. I sold clothes, furniture, every thing I had, to keep *her*, my little one, from starving, — every thing went but my wedding-ring and her hair. The wedding-ring went first ; then her beautiful curls, — yes, I curled them even when we were crying with hunger, — but it was all of no use. She died. But she's not starving *now* — thank God for that ! Not cold either ; but I can't find her — I can't see her. She went where I can't go yet. But I know this is one of her curls, and I *must* have it. That other one isn't mine. Where are the rest ? " turning fiercely to Sheniona.

" Never mind now about the rest, my good woman. They're not here, that's plain. Begone ! "

The woman, pressing the curl to her lips, moved away, and Ella saw her no more.

" Who does the other curl belong to ? " cried Sheniona. " Move quickly now. Don't be all night about it."

At these words four young girls stepped forward. One of them lifted the curl ; and, without a word, they began rapidly to untwist it. Each with busy fingers drew out strand after strand ; and when it was all divided they vanished with their treasure.

" Humph ! " exclaimed Sheniona, " if that's all, you'll be bothering me a good while before you can recover your headfuls. (A plague to these fellows with their ' sorting ' and ' lengthening,' and so scattering one lot of hair to every corner of the earth !) Ah, you thief ! "

Ella looked up quickly.

" No, not you. I'm speaking to that thing who just grabbed a braid. She's a thief and a murderer."

"I know it," sullenly retorted a woman who now stood pulling and shaking out the braid. "I was as bad as the worst. Why not? Who had any mercy for *me?* They cut off my hair in prison. Yes, a thief and a murderer. But who was any better? They murdered me on a scaffold; and they stole my hair. It was the only bright thing I ever had. "It's mine, and I want it!"

"Well, well, not so much noise, old jail-bird. Who says you can't have it?"

"*She's* said it!" retorted the woman, looking savagely at Ella. "She's claimed it for her own, and you wouldn't let me come. Haven't I seen her many a time, here, in this very room, smooth it and braid it as if God had given it to her. Yes; and haven't I seen her carrying it about in gay ball-rooms, among splendid ladies and gentlemen, with their flowers and jewels and scents, — the very hair that I used to trail in the dust? Yes; and didn't she twine it with pearl, and didn't I see a man who danced with her put a white rose-bud in it once, ha! ha! and"—

"Oh, oh! Stop her, Sheniona," cried Ella — "stop her, or I shall go mad!"

The woman, scornfully acknowledging a signal from the Spirit of the Waterfall, vanished with angry mutterings.

"Mad!" echoed a voice; "I *did* go mad, raving mad, and they cut off my locks, — 'sunny locks,' he used to call them. But that was when I lived on earth. I'm not mad now, and" — seizing another braid from Ella's lap, — "I want my hair."

"Not mad now, eh?" said the Spirit of the Waterfall. "Any one would think, from the way you act, that you were stark, staring mad."

" It's the sight of the hair does it," returned the other mournfully, and in a gentler tone. " The hair was what he always praised most."

" Who was *he?* " asked Sheniona with some interest. " Was he a barber ? "

" No, indeed," said the girl : " he was a soldier, as handsome and brave a soldier as ever breathed — noble and good too ; but you can't understand any thing about that."

" That's because I'm all in a snarl, perhaps," assented Sheniona ironically.

" But *you* can," turning to Ella. " He was so noble and good ; and when the word came that he was lying dead on the field, — lying all mangled and trodden, — I couldn't stand it. I thought I should never, never see him again. I know better now. But this hair is his because he liked it. I couldn't rest while I knew it was being carried about by others in the bustling world. I died soon after they took it. Why couldn't they lay it in my grave where it belonged ? Ah ! if you knew all, my pretty lady, you would have perished sooner than have carried my poor hair into gay houses."

" Yes, yes," sobbed Ella. " O Sheniona ! I've been so wicked, so dreadfully wicked ; but it's all your fault."

" Oh, certainly, of course ! " returned Sheniona. " You're just like all the rest. Now, ladies, if you'll be kind enough to divide the waterfall, and each take ' your own,' we can be gone. (Come, Fire, a little brighter !) "

The Fire obeyed. Instantly the girl who had been a maniac vanished ; the rest of the women seized the golden waterfall from Ella's unresisting hands, and with many struggles, exclamations, sighs, and sobs, began to tear it to pieces, and pick out "their own," hair by hair.

What strange-looking creatures they were, and dressed in what motley variety of costume! Some of them had long, wavy tresses, that had grown out since they had been shorn of their wealth ; but most of them were closely cropped, and had a weird, restless look. There were pretty, blue-eyed Bohemian girls among them, dressed in picturesque attire ; heavy Dutch lasses with great wooden shoes, that now made a strange, unearthly clatter : Swiss women with freckled faces and high caps ; and two Swedish sisters, who stamped their ghostly feet indignantly to think how their bright locks had been boiled and twisted and baked.

Some seemed to have died, and others were the spirits of the living ; but one and all were equally eager. During their rapid work they cast reproachful words or bits of personal history at Sheniona, and sometimes addressed themselves to Ella, who, with clasped hands and tearful eyes, sat wondering — a throng of new thoughts and resolutions rushing into her soul. Some told how their hair had been taken off in illness; some how they had been forced to part with theirs through poverty ; some told tales that brought a burning flush to Ella's cheek ; and others confessed that when they were working in the fields or at household duties, the hair-peddlers came along, shears in hand, and induced them to allow their tresses to be cut off in exchange for tawdry trinkets. Nearly all had something to say ; and Ella vaguely wondered that their voices seemed so lifelike and natural. If she had but thought of the potent influence of Sheniona, she would have wondered less.   Under the spell of the Spirit of the Waterfall, all things seem real.

One of the Dutch girls turned angrily toward Sheniona. "What does this mean?   I find only four hairs."

"It means that only four hairs of all your headful were fit to put with this lot," was the answer.   "It was nearly all turned to flax.   How did you fade yourself out so?"

"Ah!" said the jufvrouw, "my hair had a poor chance. I couldn't wear caps all the time; but I had one for Kermis-days.   What, with tending geese, and working on the polders, and picking hemp for the mills, there wasn't much to save my good looks.   Blazing sun and high winds, and the heavy breath of the ditches, don't go to make up fine ladies.   Where is the rest of my hair?"

"Scattered about everywhere, if you want to know," said Sheniona: "it made about twenty different shades when they came to handle and assort it.   Part of it is in a set of side-curls in London, part in a lawyer's 'scratch' somewhere in Boston, part in a mustache owned by a New Yorker who is always dodging the detectives, but most of it's on dolls."

"Dolls?"

"Yes, dolls,—those tow-headed, wax dolls.   I shouldn't be surprised if you fitted out a dozen of 'em."

"I'll find it all yet," hissed the Dutch lass between her teeth.   "I'll find it all yet."

"Not unless you're civil you wont.   Now, good people, don't stand all night disputing over one hair!"

The scene was over at last.   The "golden mass of wealth" had dwindled to nothing.   One by one the women vanished.   The fire flickered wildly, and Ella was once more alone with Sheniona.

"Don't cry," said the Spirit: "I've not deserted you yet. Tell me what I can do for you."

"Nothing, nothing!" sobbed Ella. "Only leave me, and never, never come near me again."

"Never!" repeated Sheniona, in astonishment.

"Never."

"Why, you will look like a fright."

"No," said my brave little Ella, quite herself now. "I shall *not* look like a fright. I am not bald. But for your wicked spells, I should never have slighted the adornment Nature had already given me."

"Nature!" sneered the Spirit, with intense scorn.

"It is you, Sheniona," continued Ella, "who all these months have made me look like a fright; you who have loaded my poor head till it ached; you who have made me almost a liar and a cheat; you who have made me wrong those poor women, and worry them in their graves; you who" —

"Hold!" cried Sheniona, now in a great passion. "You have said enough. From this hour I am done with you. Yes, I and my army shall withdraw from you forever!"

"Your army!"

"I have said it. — Come forth, my brave followers!" cried the Spirit of the Waterfall.

Instantly numerous boxes and drawers about the room flew open; and out hopped a regiment, it seemed, of crimpers and crinkling-pins. These were marshalled by a number of puffy officers, brevetted "rats" and "coils;" while conspicuous among them stalked a stately pair of curling-tongs.

"This way!" commanded the Spirit turning savagely about.   16

She marched toward the fireplace; her army followed in rattling procession. At the hearth she stepped upon the pan. From the pan she hopped upon the bars. From the bars she sprang into the blaze; and in the blaze she vanished, army and all.

"Thank Heaven! She's gone!" cried Ella, starting up. "But what a dreadful odor of burning! And how hot it is! Oh!"

An instant, and she was in the hall, screaming, "Help! Fire!" with all her might.

The household were awake by this time. Men were rushing in at the front door. Ella, looking back into her room, saw the toilet-table a blackened mass; saw her beautiful dress on the chair suddenly leap up in a fiery flash; saw the curtains near by curling and blazing; and realized how that star of gaslight had treacherously done its work, lighting the slow-burning damask, that in time had fired the light draperies of her toilet-table. She would have ventured in to rescue a few precious notes that were locked in her work-table; but a gruff voice shouted through the smoke, —

"Don't come in, miss!— Here, Jim, down with them curtains the first thing!"

"Mercy on us! Oh, my! oh, my!" shrieked the house-keeper, who at that instant burst upon the scene, an image of frantic despair in double-gown and night-cap. "Mercy on us! Come quick, Miss Ella, before the stairs goes!"

Thanks to prompt action and the good offices of Croton, the fire was soon arrested with scarcely more damage done than that which we have already seen. In a week or two carpenters, painters, gilders, upholsterers, and cabinet-makers had come and gone, leaving every thing as it was before.

Every thing? No, not quite. Ella was changed. No longer a victim to the spells of Sheniona, she became faultless in her beauty as she was true and tender at heart. Left to itself, her lovely hair, tossed lightly back from her temples, soon fell into a waving way of its own, beautiful to behold ; and the golden net in which her looped-up tresses were imprisoned seemed to shine with gladness because it held only Ella's hair. What a pretty trick of thoughtfulness, too, came over my little girl! Why, in her girlish wisdom she could put a dozen pompous men to shame! She became an inspiration to me, waking into healthy activity the drowsy instinct that had been disgusted with shams, yet had not strength to denounce them. She even asked me timidly one evening, whether I didn't think we'd be happier if we were to spend more time quietly together, and less in the whirl of ballrooms. Bless her heart! before long we actually read books together. Think of that! Read books, — good, sensible books too. When the time came, as it did last winter, that we had a pretty house of our own to furnish, we went out together to see about pictures : my darling is really growing to have quite an eye for that sort of thing. We bought photographs too, and a piano and a bookcase ; but the great treasure of all to me, in the furniture line, is that big armchair. If it hadn't been saved that night, I really am not sure that I would have cared to go to housekeeping.

"You foolish boy!" exclaimed Ella, the other night, when, thinking aloud, I uttered this sentiment in her presence. "You foolish, crazy boy! How can you talk such nonsense ? "

I was grave in an instant.

"Ella, dear," I said, "in my opinion that chair (incidentally, of course) changed the whole current of our lives. You know we've neither of us had one clouded moment since the night of the fire, when you fell asl" —

"Now, Willie, stop!" cried Ella, blushing tearfully. "Don't you know we were never, *never* to speak of that dreadful night again?"

Sunday Afternoon in a Poor-House.

OME persons have a way of showing their keen appreciation of pleasant conditions by rushing off in thought to their extreme opposites.

As last Sunday was a glorious day, golden with sunlight and rich with blithesome messages sent through the whispering air and written on the blue sky in cloud-white hieroglyphics, and as I was surrounded by luxury and could hear the sweet voices of a score of church-bells, my enjoyment reached such a height that I concluded to go to the Poor-House. Fortunately the mood was readily communicated to a friend. We joined hands with a true Yankee "Let's!" and started.

It was easy enough to open the Poor-House gate; easy enough to look up at the great red brick building, with its massive wings that had no thought of flying, its many windows, looking out nowhere in particular, and its Ironic order of architecture generally; easy enough to mount the steps, ring the bell; and, alack! wofully easy instantly to wish one's self a mile away. What *would* the Poor-House folk say? Who would come to the door? Would they let us in — and on Sunday?

The door opened — something rushed out. For an instant I was sure it was a crowd of paupers. But no: it was only voices, — a mingled swell of voices that suddenly ceased as we went in, as if, somehow, we had pinched it to death by shutting the door. A mild young man looked inquiringly at us, without speaking, and then motioned us to enter and go to the left. I noticed several things in a flash. In the first place, we were in a great bare hall, covered with bright oil-cloth; second, the surrounding wood-work was very white and shiny; third, the ceiling was high; and, fourth, though every thing seemed strangely silent, there was a great noise somewhere. It might have been in the air, or in the oil-cloth, or in the mild young man's eyes, I didn't exactly know. This lasted only for an instant; then I felt sure there was a crowd of persons near us, and that the noise came simply from the fact of their being alive: a voice became audible as we turned into a narrow passage-way.

Some one was praying. The rush of sound we had heard was the closing note of a hymn. There were open doors around this inner hall; through one we saw a room full of men, and at the others, strange figures of women, who were flitting about uneasily. We moved on softly, and took the chairs that the young man offered us. They were just inside the doorway of the room where the men sat. Now we could see a row or two of bare-headed women at the far-end of the apartment and all along one side. Dingy-looking men sat against the opposite wall. What revelations we saw in those rows of pauper faces!

They seemed to be mute visitors from some land of rags where the sun never shone, — to have sprung into life full grown, yet with only misery for heart-blood, so restless and desolate their look. In the centre of the room stood a table with an open Bible upon it, and around this table, several feet away from it, about a dozen well-dressed men were seated, — men with furrowed, earnest faces, restful yet anxious eyes, and nearly all of them had their hands clasped in eager interest. They were the members of the Praying Band of N——, who visit the Poor-House every alternate Sunday, and spend an hour with its inmates.

The prayer had almost imperceptibly changed to an appeal to those present. The rich, deep voice of the speaker was answered in various parts of the room with sighs of sympathy and occasional bursts of " Amen ! " " God be praised ! " " Ah, yes ! " All that he said was admirable, — no rhetorical display was needed here. He had a message of love and mercy for his hearers, and he told it simply, with tears in his eyes. " There is help for all ! " he almost sobbed, " help for all ! I have read a glorious promise for you and for me. Jesus loves you : he is knocking now at your door. Will you turn him away ? "

" No, no, God forbid ! " moaned a fervent voice. " Let him in ! let him in ! "

It came from an old woman in a faded cotton skirt and shawl : she was bent nearly double, the big ruffle on her cap flapped over a sallow little face that seemed to have neither eyes nor mouth, but only wrinkles, a chin, and a nose, — a poor, miserable little speck of a woman ; and yet how she took her place with earth's mighty ones at that moment! A human soul is grand, even in a poor-house.

Then there was a hymn, — the Doxology, — we all stood up and sang, even the bent old woman and a very aged man, who trembled as if he were afraid of falling. While we stood, the blessing was invoked, and the Praying Band, after saying a few hearty words to this one and that, went off cheerily enough, and left us alone with the overseer and the paupers.

My friend talked with the overseer; but I walked along the hall, exchanging a word or two with the women who stood around. One of the poor creatures was crazy — "harmless," they said; but she seemed tortured with inward bitterness. I smiled at her, trusting to the magnetism of kindness and sympathy; but she glowered at me with a hideous grimace that sent the blood running back icily into my heart. Then she stood aside and nodded. I tried again, offering the smile as before. How good my friends have been never openly to complain of its quality! This poor creature candidly testified her disapproval, and sent it back to me in horrible travesty. Poor creature, what has wrecked her, I wonder? There was no time to ask questions, for there was too much to be seen.

I noted one woman, whose possible history opened before me like a revelation. She was thin and gaunt, with a skin like old parchment, and a loose under lip that seemed to say sullenly, " Once I was pretty and red, and I used to smile, and say saucy things." She seemed about forty years old ; her head had great bald spots over the ears, and its little wisp of yellowish-gray hair was gathered into a knot by a broken red comb that long ago had been showy. Her dress was of a dim, nameless hue, and hung as if its life had long ago been washed away ; a once gay necker-chief was folded over her flat breast, and lying over this was a wide frill of cotton lace, gathered at the long sinewy throat. The collar evidently had been washed for Sunday ; and, strange to say, the woman, after all, had something of what is called a stylish look. There was an old-time grace lurking somewhere among her bones, ugly and faded and wretched as she was. I would have spoken to her, but she turned stiffly away, as if with a haughty sense that I did not belong to " her set." Near her stood a sad-faced German woman, who held a little girl by the hand. How much alike the two faces were, and yet one was fresh and bright, and the other wan with poverty and trouble ! In one, life showed like a dawn that threw a ruddy light on the clouds around ; in the other, it stood shrouded like a ghost behind the pale cheek and weary eye. Something about this mother and child made me ask the overseer whether they did not sometimes find good places for the inmates, where they could earn a livelihood. " Oh, yes ! " he said, " it often happens so ; and we do all we can toward getting the able-bodied ones into service. We try to send them away better men and women than they were when they came."

Just then I spied an old woman with large, dark eyes, looking rather more comfortable than the rest, though she leaned on a crutch, and her hands were badly swollen at the knuckles. She had a little room on the main floor. It had a comfortable bed in it, a chest, a table, a chair, and on its window-shelf were growing a few geraniums in pots and boxes. Just now the old woman stood in her doorway, and smiled brightly as I approached.

"Were you in at the meeting?" I asked.

"No," she answered, with a bright glance that lighted up her thin face, and deepened the flush on her ckeek, "I didn't go in. My rheumatiz wont let me sit down, when it ain't a mind to; but I stood outside here, and heerd it all."

"Well, that's better than nothing," I said, catching her cheery manner. "It's a happy thing, I am sure, for you to have these meetings."

"Oh, certain!" she answered. "Folks take heaps o' comfort out o' religion. It's beautiful to hear 'em prayin'."

This was uttered in such an outside way, that I was tempted to add, "Yes, and to pray one's self. Don't you think so?"

"Lor! yes," she answered, staring at me in that uncompromising way peculiar to paupers. "Lor! yes. I took religion two year ago, and prayin' is every thing to me."

"I knew something made you happy," I said, "because you take pains to have those geraniums growing in your window. Did you raise them yourself?"

"Oh, certain!" nodding her head and still staring. " Raised 'em, and have great luck with all such. I look at 'em when I'm doubled up with rheumatiz; but, thank the Lord, I off an' on can use some of my fingers right handy; and then I sew, which is nice, having good eyesight."

Just then a forlorn-looking man came out from the kitchen. "That's *him*," she said, shaking her head sidewise, "my husband — lost his health and broke down.

But he's a baker by trade, and when he kin, he helps with he bakin'."

"That's good," I said : " it must make both of you happier to feel that he is useful."

" My ! yes," she answered, with a superb wag of her head. "Oh! in course. It makes me quite airy and independent, it does."

Poor old woman ! Grand old pauper !

Next to the room where the services had been held, was the eating-hall. We saw the long bare tables, and women standing beside them, eating their early supper. A girl came in with a large wooden bowl, filled with slices of buttered bread. These were distributed around ; and in addition each had a tin cup filled with milk. Certainly all appeared neither under-fed nor sickly, though they wore the inevitable look that comes with long hardship, and which rarely is driven away by relief.

Next, after a few enterprising explorations, we found ourselves on a little back porch of the building, my friend and the overseer discussing points that did not interest me, and I peering about with a vague dread that I might see something which it would not be pleasant to discover.

Of course I did that very thing. Behind me was the smooth-walled hall with its shining oilcloth ; above me, the blue sky with its suggestion of bird-song ; before me, trees in which a soft breeze was sporting ; and so I peered into a kind of square area, or wall-corner, or whatever it was, and saw — what !

Two women, — one clinging to a bench, and looking more like a huge, gray, half-dead bat than a woman, so dustily flimsy were her rags and hangings; and another, at brazen-looking thing, in the very bravery of squalor. The brazen-looking thing was either an idiot or a lunatic, I could not tell which: the busy, aimless look in her face meant nothing. She seemed the guardian of the bat. Near by, where some scrubber had left it, stood a pail of dirty water with a sponge in it. Suddenly the half-witted thing stooped, and, taking the sponge from the pail, lifted it all dripping to the other woman's bowed face. There was no remonstrance, only a wretched jerk of the head, which ceased with the second stroke of the wet sponge. When for a third time it was dipped for a fresh supply, again to be aimlessly thrust into the poor helpless face, I called to the overseer; and he stopped the proceedings with a sharp "stut-t-t!" that sent the half-witted creature off to a corner, grinning, and rubbing her wrists, as though she were a monkey.

In again for further explorations, and up, up, to the very top of the building. Then after we had mounted to the cupola, which, after the manner of most cupolas, was not at that moment in a condition to afford us a "lookout," we turned, and went down again past the bed-chambers, and the sitting-rooms, dining-hall, kitchens, wash-rooms, boiler-rooms, and cellars, until we found ourselves in the open air, quite at a distance from the neat doorway by which we had entered.

Then, with many thanks, we bade our guide good-by, and sought the front gate, — my friend filled with grand, philanthropic ideas, and I bathing in a grateful sunbeam of thought, in which floated, mote-like, bathing-tubs, patent ventilators, bare tables, tin cups, a tumbled-down old man, a bald-headed, stylish pauper, a bright little child-face, the Praying Band, my "airy and independent" old woman, the dreadful creature with her sponge, and the mild young man who had let us in.

But the clouds had risen meanwhile: the air was growing chill. As I looked back at the great red building, a choking sense of human misery came over me. The brooding friend beside me was silent; and so, true to my nature, I said, —

"Let us walk fast. There'll be a bright fire at home; and they'll all be sitting round it, waiting for us."

17

Miss Malony on the Chinese Question.

CH! don't be talkin'. Is it howld on, ye say? An' didn't I howld on till the heart of me was clane broke entirely, and me wastin' that thin ye could clutch me wid yer two hands. To think o' me toilin' like a nager for the six year I've been in Ameriky — bad luck to the day I iver left the owld counthry! — to be bate by the likes o' them! (faix, an' I'll sit down when I'm ready, so I will, Ann Ryan; an' ye'd better be listnin' than drawin' yer remarks). An' is it meself, with five good charac'ters from respectable places, would be herdin' wid the haythens? The saints forgive me, but I'd be buried alive sooner'n put up wid it a day longer. Sure, an' I was the granehorn not to be lavin' at once-t when the missus kim into me kitchen wid her perlaver about the new waiter-man which was brought out from Californy. "He'll be here the night," says she. "And, Kitty, it's meself looks to you to be kind and patient wid him; for he's a furriner," says she, a kind o' lookin' off. "Sure, an' it's little I'll hinder nor interfare wid him, nor any

other, mum," says I, a kind o' stiff; for I minded me
how these French waiters, wid their paper collars and
brass rings on their fingers, isn't company for no gurril
brought up dacent and honest. Och! sorra a bit I knew
what was comin' till the missus walked into me kitchen,
smilin', and says, kind o' shcared, " Here's Fing Wing,
Kitty; an' ye'll have too much sinse to mind his bein' a
little strange." Wid that she shoots the doore; and I,
misthrustin' if I was tidied up sufficient for me fine buy
wid his paper collar, looks up, and — Howly fathers! may
I niver brathe another breath, but there stud a rale haythen Chineser, a-grinnin' like he'd just come off a tay-
box. If ye'll belave me, the crayture was that yeller it
'ud sicken ye to see him; and sorra stitch was on him
but a black night-gown over his trowsers, and the front of
his head shaved claner nor a copper-biler, and a black
tail a-hangin' down from it behind, wid his two feet stook
into the haythenestest shoes ye ever set eyes on. Och!
but I was up stairs afore ye could turn about, a-givin' the
missus warnin', an' only stopt wid her by her raisin' me
wages two dollars, and playdin' wid me how it was a Christian's duty to bear wid haythens, and taitch 'em all in our
power — the saints save us! Well, the ways and trials I
had wid that Chineser, Ann Ryan, I couldn't be tellin'.
Not a blissed thing cud I do, but he'd be lookin' on wid
his eyes cocked up'ard like two poomp-handles; an' he
widdout a speck or smitch o' whishkers on him, an' his
finger-nails full a yard long. But it's dyin' ye'd be to see
the missus a-larnin' him, an' he grinnin', an' waggin' his
pig-tail (which was pieced out long wid some black stoof,
the haythen chate!) and gettin' into her ways wonderful

quick, I don't deny, imitatin' that sharp, ye'd be shur-
prised, and ketchin' an' copyin' things the best of us will
do a-hurried wid work, yet don't want comin' to the knowledge o' the family — bad luck to him !

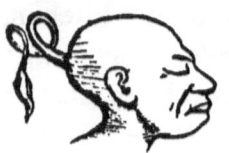 Is it ate wid him ? Arrah, an' would I
be sittin' wid a haythen, an' he a-atin'
wid drum-sticks ? — yes, an' atin' dogs an'
cats unknownst to me, I warrant ye,
which it is the custom of them Chinesers, till the thought
made me that sick I could die. An' didn't the crayture
proffer to help me a wake ago come Toosday, an' me fold-
in' down me clane clothes for the ironin', an' fill his haythen mouth wid water, an' afore I could hinder, squirrit it
through his teeth stret over the best linen tablecloth,
and fold it up tight, as innercent now as a baby, the dirrity
baste ! But the worrest of all was the copyin' he'd be
doin' till ye'd be dishtracted. It's yerself knows the tinder
feet that's on me since ever I've bin in this counthry.
Well, owin' to that, I fell into a way o' slippin' me shoes
off when I'd be settin' down to pale the praities, or the
likes o' that ; and, do ye mind, that haythen would do the
same thing after me whiniver the missus set him to parin'
apples or tomaterses. The saints in heaven couldn't ha'
made him belave he cud kape the shoes on him when he'd
be paylin' any thing.

Did I lave for that ? Faix, an' I didn't. Didn' he get
me into throuble wid my missus, the haythen ! Ye're
aware yerself how the boondles comin' in from the grocery often contains more'n 'll go into any thing dacently.
So, for that matter, I'd now and then take out a sup o'
sugar, or flour, or tay, an' wrap it in paper, and put it in

me bit of a box tucked under the ironin'-blanket the how it cuddent be bodderin' any one. Well, what shud it be, but this blessed Sathurday morn, the missus was a-spakin' pleasant an' respec'ful wid me in me kitchen, when the grocer buy comes in, and stands fornenst her wid his boondles; an' she motions like to Fing Wing (which I never would call him by that name ner any other but just haythen) — she motions to him, she does, for to take the boondles, an' empty out the sugar an' what not where they belongs. If ye'll belave me, Ann Ryan, what did that blatherin' Chineser do but take out a sup o' sugar, an' a han'ful o' tay, an' a bit o' chaze, right afore the missus, wrap 'em into bits o' paper, an' I spacheless wid shurprize, an' he the next minute up wid the ironin'-blanket, an' pullin' out me box wid a show o' bein' sly to put them in. Och, the Lord forgive me, but I clutched it, an' the missus sayin', "O Kitty!" in a way that ud cruddle your blood. "He's a haythen nager," says I. "I've found yer out," says she. "I'll arrist him," says I. "It's yerself ought to be arristed," says she. "Yer won't," says I. "I will," says she. And so it went, till she give me such sass as I cuddent take from no lady, an' I give her warnin', an' left that instant, an' she a-pointin' to the doore.

17*

LITTLE TALKS.

BY SUSAN SNAPP.

OUR DEBATING SOCIETY SKELETON.

HERE'S a skeleton in every house," says some old growler ; and it's true. John and I managed to keep ours away for a long time, but we knew it would turn up at last. Sure enough, it's come ! It has only got as far as our Debating Society as yet ; whether it ever gets any further, or not, is a matter of single combat between it and John.

Now, if Mr. Snapp shines anywhere, it is in debate, The opposing side always loses heart as soon as he begins, He makes a point of being master of his subject, never loses his temper, and invariably throws the balance in favor of his own side of a question. I don't say this be- cause he's my John — not at all. If he couldn't debate well, I'd be sure to know it, for we often take up little questions between ourselves. Besides, I'm always so anxious when he rises to speak in public, that my whole soul listens. Consequently his weak points, if there are any, always strike me with tremendous force, though that may be rather a contradictory way of putting it.

I'm not the only one who holds this opinion. The whole town thinks the same. They always try to have two or three extra speakers, " to balance Snapp " as they say ; or, rather, they did so until our skeleton appeared at the Debating-Society meetings, — a real skeleton, with a skin drawn over it, and called by courtesy a man. Yes, he's a plain, gaunt, high-shouldered, long-nosed old farmer, who carries a red bandanna, and talks through his nose, with a most atrocious twang beside ; one of your perverse, aggravating creatures, who utters about six words a day, and sets you foaming. This old fellow has attended but two of our meetings ; and already he's turned every thing inside out and topsy-turvy — that is, as far as John's position is concerned. The first time he came — shall I ever forget it ? — he sat in the darkest corner of the old schoolhouse, taking a nap through the greater portion of the debate. At last John's turn came ; and, in the pleasant rustle and stir that always take place when John rises to speak, our skeleton woke up.

Well, John spoke beautifully, if I *do* say it. The question was, " Which has the Greater Effect upon Mankind, — Hope, or Fear ? " Luckily John was on the Hope side, which, having good sense, religion, and poetry with it, made his task as inspiriting as it was easy. The other side had been cleverly sustained. Collins's Ode on the Passions had been quoted with great effect ; but it was really wonderful to see John carry his audience away from the point where his opponent, an eloquent young college graduate, had left them shuddering.

No : Fear was low, Hope was high ; Fear was cowardice, Hope was courage ; Fear was this, Hope was that ; and so on, until even those on the opposite side, forgetting their defeat, grew radiant. As for me, I could hear the Bow-bells of my ambition saying, "Turn again, Snapp, member of the Legislature." At last, after asserting something about Hope springing eternal in the human breast, he gave a peroration that made me say "Dear old John " under my breath, and —

Up jumped the skeleton.

No ; he didn't jump up at all. He just slowly stretched his neck upward, and kept on until it brought him standing. Then he looked about him with such an air ! It was not conceit, nor assurance, and certainly it was not meekness ; it struck me as being more of an anti-John air than any thing else — but I may have been mistaken.

"Ladies and gentlemen," said he, through his nose, " I didn't come here to-night with any notion of speakin', nor hev I any thin' pertickerlar to say except on one p'int. The question is, whether Hope or Fear has the greatest effect upon mankind ; and how have you decided it ? "

" Hope has it," exclaimed a voice.

" That's so," said another.

" Order ! " shouted the chairman.

" I go in for Hope," cried a daring young fellow near the door.

Thereupon a timid friend of the other side essayed a faint "Fear."

Instantly the place was in what may be called an orderly uproar. Scores of voices shouted " Hope ! Hope ! " and, at every faint solo of "Fear," the Hope chorus gathered strength and audacity.

Meantime I nudged John proudly ; and he looked benignly at the chairman, as if to say, —

"The audience is slightly won over, you see."

The skeleton coughed. Instantly the voices went out as if they had been lights.

"So do I go in for Hope," he twanged, — "go in for it most entire ; but that hain't the p'int under discussion. The question is, which has the greatest influence upon man? Now, I calc'late you can't affect a man any more serious than to kill him."

"That's so," responded somebody aloud, and everybody mentally.

"Very well," drawled the old fellow, beginning to sit down, and finishing his sentence just as he touched the seat ; "there's lots o' instances of men and women dyin' of fear, but who ever heerd of any one a-dyin' of hope?"

Poor John ! What chance had he with a country audience after that? The vote was taken at once, and FEAR carried it almost unanimously.

Then the subject for the next debate was proposed and accepted : —

"Which has proved the Greater Blessing to the Human Race, — Literature or Agriculture?"

The sides were given out ; and as good luck would have it, John was put down for Agriculture, and the skeleton was made the champion of Literature !

This was too good a joke to be passed by. Everybody laughed except the skeleton. He merely stuffed his bandanna into his hat, put it on, and walked out like a somnambulist.

I *was* worked up, I confess. The idea of John, who is nothing more nor less than pure gold, being made to appear like German silver by a creature like that ! However, I said nothing, but waited for the next meeting.

It came off last week, and, like Tam O'Shanter —
though, I'm glad to say, in a different way — John was
glorious. He put Literature on a very little shelf in less
than no time ; but Agriculture he made to shine as the
second sun of the universe, — Agriculture, the great feeder
and ennobler of man. Literature seemed generally weak
that night. Its seven advocates took it out mainly in
coughing, and saying, " Mr. Chairman ; " but nearly every
man and woman there knew the blessings of a farmer's
life, — its freedom, its pride of honest toil, its slow but
sure rewarding.

Four of the advocates of Agriculture excelled themselves. They were nearly as good as John ; but then, you
see, their subject gave them every advantage, especially
as all who had spoken on the other side were country
bumpkins, and didn't know an epic from an almanac.
There was but one speaker left for them, and that was the
skeleton, who, of course, would flounder helplessly if he
attempted to ford this question.

At last he rose ; and I assure you, his side didn't " die
of hope " when he began.

" Friend Scott has called upon me to say somethin'"
said he, after his neck had pulled him to his feet ; " but it
don't hardly seem worth while."

[" Aha ! " hissed my revengeful heart, and even John
smiled grimly.]

" I hain't an argermentative man, myself," he continued,
" and I don't hold to take part in these 'ere debates ; but
I do hold that this is a good Christian assembly, and it
does go ag'in me to see what the Almighty entailed on
man as a curse bein' held up in this 'ere place as a
blessin'." 18

Down he sat. The audience, sound and orthodox to a man, ahemmed, hawed, and, I need not say, passed a unanimous vote on the side of the skeleton : even John held up his right hand for Literature.

That's all. I don't know that any thing can be done about it. Setting aside slang, which I abhor, my only hope is, that, as the old fellow hasn't more than a pint of blood in him, he may dry up before long, and disappear.

SUNSHINE.

EELING rather blue to-day, it occurs to me to say something about sunshine. A good idea! Already the blessed word shows brightly upon the paper. Its alliteration seems to appeal directly to me. " Sun, Susan! Shine, Snapp!" it says in brisk, peremptory tones ; and why shouldn't I try? It will be better for John, for the children, for the servants, for all of us.

Shine in here, please, good Sun, and let us find out what's the matter. Ah! I see. A little discontent, a little laziness, a little selfishness, and a moiety of that vague feeling of apprehension which loves to steal in upon one unawares. Why, I thought it was some real trouble! Already the wee, restless motes are floating off in the bright beams, and I am happy. My prayer without words is answered. How beautiful every thing is out of the window, — the sky, the trees, the grass, even the flower-beds that need weeding, and the garden-paths gullied afresh by last night's rain! It is pleasant, after all, to see so much out-of-door work to be done. It gives one a familiar fellowship with Nature, a sort of tussling, you-and-I feeling, that adds vastly to one's sense of importance.

Glancing roomward from the window, the view still is pleasant. There's a home look about things, though the armchair does need a new cushion. (So there is Dick! Sing away! What! jolly, and in prison? There, I'll put you in the sun too.)

Dick likes that. Ah! how he sings now! I never thought of it before; but really that trill is just full to the brim of household names. As I listen, I can hear them all — not distinctly, but strangely blended in a few shrill, ecstatic notes. Is the sunshine on the carpet really quivering, or do I fancy it? No, it's the shadow of Dick's fairy cage, as he hops about and makes it swing. Looking at the sunshine — that giver of life, health, and joy — reminds me of a true story that never has been printed.

Dear little Kitty G—— used to live next door with her widowed mother and a very irritable grandfather, who — poor old man! — couldn't bear the play of children, and always, in chiding them, let his aches and pains get the better of his once cheery voice. Kitty, with her floating, golden-brown hair, her blue eyes and dimpled little shoulders, looked too pretty a thing to growl at; yet he *would* growl often at the mere sound of her voice. At other times he would sit silent for hours, scowling darkly, and seeming to have wilfully stalked away from all warmth and kindliness. Strange to say, little Kitty had certain ways so like his that they really alarmed her mother. The child often would become moody without a cause, or go off into shocking fits of baby-passion. Her health seemed excellent; her eyes were bright, and her cheeks rosy, even when the "grandfather look," as the household called it, was settling upon her face. Various plans of cure were tried in vain. At last, during one of Kitty's worst spells of sullenness, a sudden inspiration came to the poor mother.

The sunshine was streaming into the room.

"Kitty," she said, moving a tiny rocking-chair to a brightly lighted spot on the carpet, "come sit here a little while."

The child obeyed in angry silence.

"What you want me to sit here for?" she snapped forth after a few moments' waiting.

"Because it is such a glad place, Kitty. The sun is shining there, all the way from heaven."

"I don't care!" is Kitty's irreverent comment.

"*I* care," answers the mother softly; "for the sun makes the world light and the waters bright. It puts color into birds, flowers, butterflies, and every thing. It brings gladness and new life to the world every morning. It comes from God, Kitty; and I pray that He will let some of its brightness and gladness steal into you."

Instantly Kitty jerked her chair aside, out of the bright beam, as if resolved that no unfair advantage should be allowed, and again muttered, "I don't care."

The mother made no reply. She could not, for the tears that were welling up in her heart. Still Kitty rocked and scowled, holding her pretty blue dress and white apron close to her side, as if to keep it entirely out of the sunlight. Meantime her eyes were fixed defiantly upon the bright spot on the floor.

Suddenly she looked up in amazement.

"Mamma," she cried, "it's creepin'—it's comin' to Kitty!"

18*

"That's because God loves you," said the mother, trembling, yet not knowing why. "Oh ! if my little girl would only let the sun come to her straight from God, it would brighten her, I know: all the ugly shadows would run out of her heart."

Kitty did not answer: she was watching the bright spot. In her eagerness, she slid from her chair, and knelt upon the carpet. The light crept nearer, nearer; it touched the hem of her dress, it climbed up her little apron, it folded her in its splendor, it danced in her eyes ; and she burst forth into a happy, childish laugh.

"It's come, mamma !" she cried joyfully. "It's come!" "Don't cry, mamma !" she said coaxingly, as her mother, kneeling beside her, kissed her again and again. "Don't cry, mamma ! I dess Kitty wont never be naughty any more."

"My own darling, I am so glad ! Wont you thank God, Kitty, for all this ? "

"I *dess* I will," said the little girl, as if deliberating upon it ; "p'rhaps I'll put something about it in my 'Now I lay me,' to-night, because I do like the funny old sun. — Now, you rocking-chair, you must go back to the wall, mustn't you ? "

So, childlike, happy, and full of loving pranks, the little one spent the rest of the long day in a manner that astonished all the household, accustomed as they had been to her almost hourly fits of gloom and ill-humor. That night, as she kissed her mother for good-night, the rosy mouth lingered a moment to whisper, "How shall I thank Dod about that ? "

Sunlight had indeed entered her soul. To be sure, the

naughty spells were not gone entirely ; but the intervals between them grew longer and longer, and each time they were checked in nearly the same way. The little creature would willingly sit or stand in the sunshine, at her mother's suggestion; and good-humor would come almost instantly. Once, on a rainy day, when she felt her temper rising, she said suddenly, " Oh ! if Kitty is naughty now, she can't det back ; can she, mamma ? " And mamma laughed, told her a pretty story, cooed a sweet song in her ears, — any thing to take the sunshine's place, — until the little heart grew bright again.

But this is not the end of the story. Months passed. The old grandfather evidently was failing : he would sit in his chair now nearly all day without noticing any one, except to mutter ill-humoredly when addressed. One beautiful morning his frown was even darker than usual. Kitty stole into the room with a hatful of cherries, and ventured to offer him some. His sharp rebuff sent the child trembling to her mother's side. For a moment they both looked wistfully at the poor old man, but the incident was too common to surprise them long. Soon Kitty had slipped away, and Mrs. G—— was sewing as busily as ever.

At last something caused the mother to raise her head.

There stood Kitty, near the south window, the sunlight streaming full upon her, lighting her bright hair, her eager, upturned face, and her apron, which she held up at the corners, with her chubby little arms extended.

It was a beautiful picture ; and it stood so still, it might easily have been taken for a picture in reality.

" What are you doing, Kitty ? " asked the mother at last.

" I'm catchin' sunshine to t'row over dran'pa," said Kitty.

The old man leaned back in his chair with an amused smile. Then, as the child began to move very slowly and cautiously toward him, he watched her with interest. Suddenly she stopped short, with a pitiful, "O mamma! it wont stay. It's all spilling out. — Dran'pa, dran'pa! you'll have to come here quick." And with an eager cry she caught up the apron, with its little remnant of sunlight, and hugged it to her breast. The grandfather smiled again, and was almost tempted to rise ; but Kitty was too delighted to wait. In a moment she had rushed to him, and he was lifting her to his lap, while she hurriedly opened her apron to toss the sunshine into his face.

Did it stay there ? Yes, it did ; for somehow grandfather never was really cross to Kitty after that day.

MIGRATORY HUSBANDS.

NEVER had one of them, thank heaven! but I know they must be dreadful, — these heads of families who are forever popping up in new localities, with a "Lo! I'll build here. Here's a rising bit of property;" or, "This old cottage I'll renovate, clap on a wing and a piazza, live in it six months, and sell out at a bargain." Then those husbands who are forever shifting their business from place to place, — now to a village, now to a city, now to the backwoods, — a delightful time must their wives have of it! Never mind how faithful, devoted, and enterprising a woman may be, it's a great trial for her to be continually pulling up stakes, and tearing away home-tendrils, even if her migratory spouse is in other respects the best in the world. I'd like to see the person who would tell me that I wouldn't go with John, if he decided to set up a soda-fountain in the Desert of Sahara. No. I'd go; but I should suffer in the going, though I told my woes not even to old Cheops himself. But what if, instead of one grand move, he flitted about like a grasshopper? What if he tried Bloomfield, and Flatbush, and Woodside, and Harlem, and a dozen other places, from the coming of the first nursery-tooth to the going away of the last nursery-measles? What if he dipped the children into twenty schools, filled every April air with mournful farewells to all our neighbors, and kept the parlor carpets in a perpetual spasm of contraction and expansion? Could I be the blessed, happy woman that I am? Shouldn't I be thin, weary, and heart-sore, and the children morally just little waifs made of the shreds and patches of many villages? Certainly. Far be it from me to question established similes of wifehood: but your oaks don't hop about. They stand still and give the clinging vines a chance to take root beside them.

Only yesterday, while shopping in town, I chanced to find myself in a street-car beside a man and a stout woman engaged in earnest conversation. His was a thin, flushed face, with restless eyes, and lips that asked "Why?" "Who?" "Where?" even when they were silent. Hers was soft, fleshy, massive; and its little eyes were full of temporary affability and interest. He evidently was speaking of some recent bereavement, while the lady leaning toward him wore a sort of wash of deep feeling which was "not a dye," though it gave her a hue of sympathy quite proper in a street-car. Presently I caught the words, —

"She was in-deed. You lost a treasure when you lost *her.*"

"Yes, and a wonderful creature for moving about," pursued the man, with deep feeling. "It didn't make any difference: you could take that woman, and *set her down anywhere!*"

His eyes filled with tears; and I looked out of the

window, sorry for his sake, but glad that the angels had taken at least one poor woman away from a migratory husband.

The country abounds with these naturalized Bedouins. I say nothing against men who go North, South, East, or West, and settle. They are the nerves of the body politic, and indispensable to our new civilization. But I do feel impelled to quote mother's favorite expression, and whisper to hundreds of men within hearing distance at this moment, "Do stay put." For the sake of wives, home, children, yourselves, take root somewhere. Help to build up in America the beautiful homestead feeling common to Europeans, and almost unknown to us. Let your very saplings understand that in time they are to shade your great-great-grand-children.

Up with the Times.

JOHN and I have had a visitor, — a man who is up with the times. He's gone now, and we're pretty well, thank you. This very morning he waved an unsubdued farewell to his friends from the deck of an out-ward-bound steamer slowly gliding down the bay. But he was at our cottage yesterday, and the day before, and the days before that, away back to the dim, distant morning when first he appeared, valise in hand. Ask the walls if it isn't so.

Did we enjoy the visit? Certainly. I don't think John and I ever had a happier moment than when, after saying "good-by" a dozen times, we went back into the cottage, sank heavily upon the nearest chairs, and stared breath-lessly at each other.

"He's gone, John," I gasped, "and I like him."

"Yes," panted my spouse; "capital fellow is Hobkins, — such company! Been here a fortnight, hasn't he?"

"Sakes!" exclaimed Aunt Betsey, passing through the room at that moment, "if you two are not com-plete-ly worn out!"

I smiled feebly in reply; and John, simply remarking

that there were no two words about it, it really did people good to have a thorough waking up once in a while by men like Hobkins, tumbled over upon the sofa, and was soon fast asleep.

To understand the situation, one must know Hobkins. He is one of your thoroughly posted men. He is a constant reader of every thing. He knows John Doe's mother, and Richard Roe's grandfather. A false quotation sets his teeth on edge. He whisks an encyclopædia on every eyelash. He goes to the roots of things, yet knows all about the last leaf on the outermost branches. You'd think, to hear him talk, that he heard Beecher, Adams, Bellows, Cuyler, Chapin, Spurgeon, Brigham Young, and Moody preach every Sunday, and that he went everywhere and saw everybody and every thing every evening of his life.

And yet he doesn't pretend, or put on airs. He simply inhales the events of the day, and breathes them out personally. His oxygen comes to him in paragraphs. He flashes items. His very boots creak with facts. His "good-morning" is a sort of universal preface, and his "good-night" a general "to be continued." *I* call him a man in fifty volumes ; and John says it's a silly idea, but that, while I'm about it, I may as well make it a hundred.

How the creature ever has time to wash and dress is a mystery to me. Yet his toilet is perfect. It seems as if he must force knowledge in with his hair-brush, and rub in definite ideas with his towel — yes, and grind in words with his tooth-brush. I never saw such a man !

Mr. Snapp prides himself on always being able to see both sides of an argument ; Hobkins turns the simplest question into a dodecahedron. He is so plausible, too! every illustration fits. He was born, so to speak, with a silver "why and wherefore " in his mouth. It makes no difference what you think : you'll agree with Hobkins if you live to hear the end of his statements and demonstrations.

Dear me! How much John and I know just from being with him a fortnight ; or, rather, what vistas have been opened to us, with Hobkins always standing at the far end! Sometimes he would clinch the universe in his fist, and hammer it into our centre-table for us to examine at leisure ; and sometimes I actually had to take hold of my chair, he made the world spin by so fast. One day, when he chanced to allude incidentally to his wife, I almost swooned. Mercy on us! the idea of having that man for a husband! I'd sooner marry the British Museum, and done with it. No : all the New York, Boston, Philadelphia, San Francisco, New Orleans, and European newspapers represent him more fitly. His wife must feel like a Mrs. Associated Press.

Hobkins gave us so many new ideas! Woke us up, as it were. Only to-day I got a letter from Mrs. de Kuyster, secretary of the half-orphan society, signed "Yours, etc., Mary de Kuyster." Now, what did she mean by that? A week ago I might not have noticed it, but Hobkins has been among us. Was she too lazy, too proud, or too conscientious, to tell me exactly in what way I was hers? or was the " etc." resorted to as a cowardly detour from candor? Why didn't she sign herself simply Mary de Kuyster, or " Yours moderately," " Yours somewhat," or even "Disrespectfully yours "? Any form would be preferable

to that paltry *et cætera*. I find myself vexed, not with
Mrs. de Kuyster especially, but at the custom which per-
mits these senseless impertinences. It's all wrong, this
having to say, "Your — something," for courtesy's sake,
whether it's true or not. Like "All send love," "Yours
truly" is often just bosh, — mere sentiment without a
backbone of fact. Ah! the shams that have knelt in the
closing words of letters! the downright lies that have
stridden forth in "Your humble servant," who is always
respectfully or cordially somebody's!

You should have seen Hobkins at our table. I'd no
idea plain diet could be so suggestive. He found spec-
trum analyses in the salt-cellars, international rowing-
matches in the spoons, balloon-travelling in the omelet,
and co-operative housekeeping in the hash. He drew
"survival of the fittest" from the very cheese; and, as
John confidentially remarked, actually shook kindergar-
tens and juvenile delinquents out of the baby's feeding-
apron. He found prison-discipline in the bread; and
female colleges, universal suffrage, and bland opinions
generally, in the butter. The calves-head soup brought
forth capital punishment; the beef, labor-union systems;
and the dessert was full of Gates Ajar and spiritual mani-
festations. Once, while filling his teacup, I felt as if I
were pouring out the entire Suez Canal, and I'm sure I
often dropped in a railroad accident with the sugar. What
with iron cars, and elastic platforms, and wide gauges, and
new brakes, car-starters, and compensating expansible
rail-joinings, I grew confused in spite of myself.

Really, I've not used so many big words in an age of
Sundays. Some of them were new to me two weeks ago;

but now I'd like any one to show John and me any thing of which we haven't some sort of an inkling.

Talking of ink, Hobkins says they've invented a substitute for the present tedious process of writing, which, after all, *is* a primitive and barbarous method. And, by the way, speaking of barbarous things, what an absurd idea is now going the rounds of the English and French papers, though one of our countrymen started it!—that the Americans are fast going back to Indian characteristics. They say it even of Americanized foreigners; so that in a few generations here, a Dutch face comes out with high cheek-bones, piercing eyes, straight black hair, and an expression like Big Thunder.

Talking of thunder, Hobkins is delighted with Mr. Quimby's practical ideas on self-protection during thunderstorms. He says *he* will have in future a long iron chain trailing to the ground from his summer umbrella, never mind who laughs. By the way, talking of Quimby and electricity, Hobkins says Benjamin Franklin was a brick, if he *did* wear costly laces when he wrote Poor Richard's Almanac.

Talking of bricks, perhaps you may not know that the Bricklayers' Association of New York has just —

Horror! I'm growing to be like Hobkins! I must stop.

He's a capital fellow, though, and good company; only John and I have come to the conclusion that we really can't stand having another visitor yet awhile.

March. What it has Done for Us.

BY HOBKINS.

———————◆———————

[Talking of Hobkins, John happened one day to speak of somebody having been born in the month of March. Straightway Hobkins opened a dis-
course, which, biographically and chronologically, surpassed any thing I have
ever heard. In fact, John was so favorably impressed, that our guest promised to "work the thing up evenings." He did so, and here is the result.
The wonder to me is, that Hobkins was able to follow the same trail of
research so steadily. No doubt he was stimulated by the difficulties arising
from a conflict of authorities. It is needless to say that John and I were
delighted; but somehow we were careful, during the rest of Mr. Hobkins's
visit, not to mention any other month by name. — S. S.]

IN the good old times, when wolves thought nothing
of taking princes to nurse, and the ingratitude
of republics was undreamed of, there were fewer
spokes in the year's revolving wheel than now; or, at
least, men counted them differently. Romulus, who, as
everybody knows, introduced the Roman calendar, with its
ten spokes, very properly named the first Martius, or March,
after his respected father, the god of war. Then came
added months and re-modellings, from Julius Cæsar down,
until 1752, when the *new style* was adopted in England,
and January was made the first month of the twelve.

However this arrangement may have served to lessen discrepancies between the calendar and the true solar year, I am sorry March could not have maintained the place given it by Romulus. Verily his reckoning was inspired by Nature herself ; for is not March the first, the waking month, the resurrection of the dead year ? Does she not start the forest into leaf and song, with her rushing tide of air and sunshine ? Does she not chase away the snow-drifts, and set the brooks running, and powder the soil with busy, invisible fingers, that the seed may send down its tender roots ? Does she not whistle her shrill summons to the birds, and startle the drowsy insects into life? Of course she does. Therefore, in Nature's almanac, March shall be *first* to the end of time. As she rushed through the seven-hilled city ages ago, she sweeps through our midst to-day, crying, " Arise, arise I the spring is come I "

There are other good reasons why March should make some little commotion when she visits the earth. We should bluster twice as loudly with one-half the cause. Few months can show such a record as hers. Many a March victory, a March discovery, a March invention, has left the world richer than it was before. She has ushered in some of the noblest lives humanity has ever known ; and, in God's time, has brought the final summons to those who left an undying name behind them.

To be sure, there have been black sheep in her flocks ; but by that same blackness we can trace their fleece, be it never so finely spun, through the woof and warp of history. Whether the March weaving started or ended their course, they belong to her record. Perhaps, when her voice is shrillest, when she goes screaming distractedly through the fields and forests, she is telling of them ; just as, when she bends in grand, majestic whisperings to the sunshine, she may be saying, " Angelo was one of my children. I carried Beethoven to heaven."

Not a day in March but has its story to tell : if idle in one year, it is busy in another. Let us take up each in turn, and learn what we can.

On the FIRST of March, 1469, William Caxton, at the request of the queenly Margaret, Duchess of Burgundy, commenced translating the " Recuyell of the Historyes of Troye." This remarkable work met with great favor in England ; and its large sale in manuscript copies, being at best slow and unsatisfactory, led to his putting it in type, — the first English[1] book that ever was printed.

The opening number of Addison's " Spectator " came in 1711, on the 1st of March ; and so, in 1483, did a very different order of spectator, Francis Rabelais, who doubtless saw more, thought more, and jested more, than any fifty other Frenchmen of his day.

On the SECOND, in 1791, died Wesley, the founder of Methodism. On its anniversary, six years afterward, Horace Walpole, "slave of elegant trifles," yielded up his breath. It was on the 2d, in 1848, that Louis Philippe and his queen escaped from France, and sought shelter on British shores. Another 2d of March, long ago, sent a man-child into England, destined to become a bright ornament during the golden days of Elizabeth, and to leave the Bodleian Library as his monument upon earth.

---

[1] English, though really printed in Bruges. Very rare copies of this work are still to be seen; one of them was sold, many years ago, at the Roxbury sale, for £1,060.

On the THIRD, in 1632, George Herbert, he who sang, —

" Sweet day ! so cool, so calm, so bright," —

verified his own, " all must die ; " and, on the 3d, came
two sweet-voiced poets into England, — in 1605, Edward
Waller, the smoothest singer of his day; and, forty-six
years later, Thomas Otway, famous in dramatic verse.

The FOURTH of March has had honorable work on hand
many a time since our own national life began ; but, above
all, that of 1865 stands apart, consecrated to a memory.

On the FIFTH, in 1827, Laplace, the great philosopher,
was ushered into that world whose mysteries even his
piercing gaze had not been able to penetrate ; and on the
5th, centuries before, Correggio was suddenly summoned
to behold, in all its fulness, the grandeur and beauty that
he had yearned to embody while on earth.   But the man
of many greatnesses had come earlier.   In 1474, the 6th
brought a tiny hand into the world, that afterwards produced those masterpieces of art, — the works of Michael
Angelo.

March the EIGHTH, 1817, is identified with the birth of
Layard, explorer of the antiquities of Nineveh, and with
the death of two kings, — William III. of England, in 1702,
and Bernadotte of Sweden, in 1844.

The NINTH, in 1792, brought forth William Cobbett, the
most obstinate politician, the stanchest lover of agriculture, that ever lived.   More than a century before, it had
taken away a very different politician, Richelieu's pupil,
the famous Cardinal Mazarin, slave of ambition, lover of
art, and a man so wedded to appearances that he literally
dressed for his death, so that his corpse might be well

shaven and *rouged.* In 1825, the 9th brought summons
to a gentler victim, the venerable Mrs. Barbauld, after she
had devoted nearly fifty years of her long life to the in-
struction and entertainment of the young.

The TENTH was noted, some two thousand years ago, for
being the date of an interesting surgical operation, viz.,
amputation of the head, performed upon one Helioga-
balus; a complicated case of imperial villany. Men have
nearly forgotten it now: the remedy has become less
novel; and, besides, more interesting events have come
to pass on the 10th, such as the birth of Playfair the natural philosopher, in 1748; of William Etty the painter, in
1787; and, in 1820, the death of Benjamin West, the
American President of the Royal Academy.

Torquato Tasso, one of the greatest of Italian poets, in
turn the pet and victim of Duke Alphonso of Ferrara,
was born on the ELEVENTH of March, 1544.

On the TWELFTH, in 1684, came Bishop Berkeley, the
philosopher, now chiefly remembered on account of his
pet theory, — the non-existence of matter; though his
scheme of Christianizing the savages of America, and
his persevering attempt to carry it out, show the man
in a truer and nobler light.

The THIRTEENTH, in 1681, gave birth to a little English
girl, whose name is recorded, in her parish church in
Surrey, as Esther Johnson; but to this day the world will
insist upon calling her Stella, and all because of one Jona-
than Swift, who loved her cruelly. Fifty-two years afterwards, on the same day, came the renowned Dr. Priest-
ley, he of the English cradle and American grave, whose
philosophical writings extend to nearly eighty volumes.

Among those who *went* on the thirteenth, I find the well-known names of Belisarius in A.D. 565 ; and, passing over many centuries, La Fontaine, prince of fable-writers, Mignard, the eminent French painter (both in 1695), and, in 1711, Boileau, who was considered almost a dunce till he was thirty, and then electrified France by his poetry, his wit, his sparkling companionship.   On March 13, 1845, Regina Maria Roche, author of " Children of the Abbey," opened the eternal Book of Mysteries, which all who die shall read ; and on the same day, just nine years later, departed Thomas Noon Talfourd, the never-to-be-forgotten author of " Ion."

Ninety-five years ago, on this same day of March, a lone watcher of the skies saw a new planet swim into his ken.   It was William Herschel ; and the planet was Uranus, or, as he named it, the Georgium Sidus.

The FOURTEENTH, in 1803, took Klopstock, the great German poet, away from a world that had used him more fairly than it generally uses men of genius ; and the same day, nearly fifty years before, saw Admiral Byng led out to die, in punishment for his having, as Voltaire said, "not gone near enough to a French admiral to whom his country required him to give battle."

March FIFTEENTH stands immortal in the records of the past ; for on that day, on the ides of March, forty-four years before the Christian era, Julius Cæsar, the greatest man of all antiquity, gathered his mantle about him, and fell.   What must his dying glance have been to *one* among that crowd of murderers, if to this day, " Et tu, Brute ! " gives humanity a pang !

*   *   *   *   *   *   *   *   *   *   *

The calends, the nones, the ides — how strange and unmeaning the words to us! Yet, in the old Roman times, all public events, all household changes, weddings, births, festivities, and funerals, were registered according to one or another of these leading divisions of the month. An event occurring on the 1st of March, for instance, was dated the *calends*, the first or *call* day; if later, then as so many days before the *nones*, or ninth; if later still, by giving the number of days before or after the *ides*.

Thus each item of news had its sounding phrase. The little Flavius Augustus possibly cut his first tooth on the fourth before the nones of June; his sister Antonia, it may be, went with young Aurelius to the Games on the calends of April; and their noble uncle Caius Strabo (no relation to the historian) died at twilight on the ides of November.

This last date would be styled by us November 13; for it was only in October, March, May, and July, that the ides fell upon the fifteenth of the month.

We have remembered how, on the ides of March, ages ago, Brutus and his fellow-conspirators did violence to the noblest life of all antiquity. I am reminded now of one who, in our own generation, died a peaceful death on a 15th of March, and was laid to rest in an old Italian church, beside the grave of Torquato Tasso. This is Mezzofanti of Bologna, probably the most remarkable linguist the world has ever known. There was scarcely a tongue, living or dead, that he did not master. It is said, that at the age of fifty he was proficient in as many languages as he had lived years; and, before he died, he was well acquainted with seventy. Think of a man who could read or converse fluently, not only in Latin and Greek, in English, French, German, Italian, Spanish, Dutch, and Portuguese, but also in Chinese, Russian, Turkish, Sanscrit, Coptic, Ethiopian, Abyssinian, and Sabaic, and scores of other languages and dialects, the very names of which would sound as unfamiliar to us as their own idioms ! Lord Byron once described him as " a walking polyglot, a monster of languages, and a Briareus of parts of speech." It seems to me, that, since life at the best is short, to have spoken and studied in all his tongues, he could have been little else than a human Tower of Babel.

And now, passing the ides of March, we must deal briefly with the remainder of the month ; for its days are rich with chronicled events, and with names already blazoned in the annals of fame.

Archbishop Cranmer, who, but for the fickleness of that afflicted widower Henry VIII., would possibly never have become eminent, and, but for the fidelity of the same many-sided monarch, would never have lived to call young Edward his king, was burned at the stake in March, 1556. Many a noble head has touched the block in this same eventful month. March has brought many a monarch into the world ; and to many it has brought death, — sometimes rudely, sometimes with merciful gentleness. We know how Pompey, son-in-law of Cæsar, triumvir of Rome, and only second among the conquerors of his day, fled at last, a hunted fugitive, into Egypt, and was murdered there two days after the ides of March, B. C. 45 ; how Nero fell by his own guilty hand just one hundred and thirteen years from that day ; and how, on the 23d of March, 1369, a new Cain rose up on Spanish soil to slay that black-hearted tyrant, Peter the Cruel.

We know how the summons came to James the First in March, 1625, leaving his double crown to a head that sat firmly enough on its shoulders then ; and who does not remember that royal death-bed on the 24th of March, 1603, from which Elizabeth of England went forth sceptre-less and unattended into the unknown land ?

March gave us Raffaelle in 1483,[1] and Vandyck in 1599. The birthday (22d) of the latter is richer since 1822 ; for it marks the years of Rosa Bonheur. Seven days later comes the anniversary of Thorwaldsen's death in 1844 ; and on the last of the month, in 1837, that of Constable, noted among the landscape-painters of England.

To Beethoven and Haydn also, March gave the same birthday ; for on the 31st, in 1732, Haydn was born into this life ; and on the 31st, in 1827, Beethoven was born into heaven. One year before, Von Weber had left the world his "last waltz ; " and on March 2, in 1854, the matchless voice of Rubini was stilled forever.

In the course of the research necessary in giving March her due, one truth has manifested itself which would have been invaluable to Buckle.

March is lavish in bringing fresh and beautiful impulses to Nature. There is no death in her touches here — only life ; life in tree and shrub and blade ; life in the quickened sunshine, in the very stones, in old logs and timbers, in the stirring pavement of the woods! But with mankind she is less prodigal in her gifts ; indeed, more inclined

---

[1] Some authorities say April. — *S. S.*

to rob than to enrich. Though she often has sent rare lives into the world, she oftener does the same work among mortals that her good sister November does to the fields, — blights them for a fresher blooming. Her glorious cradles are fewer than her honored graves.

Let there be no misunderstanding: I mean to cast no slur upon March babies in general. Millions and millions of these there have been, all astonishing in their way, each more remarkable than any before, — in fact, the very paragons of babyhood ; but somehow their names flourish in the family record rather than in the biographical dictionary. Their waxen, baby fingers may have tugged at the very heartstrings of their household, (God be praised for that same !) but the pioneer axes of progress, the tillers of government, the torches that light humanity through the darkness, but few of them have grasped. Therefore I repeat, March, as a rule, does not show her strength in her cradles.

There have been some famous ones, however, in which lay folded nearly all that is great or possible in humanity, whether for good or evil. If you are willing to stride over a century now and then, we can take a hasty peep into some of the cradles of the past.

First of all, see Ovid lying asleep through his first daylight, March 20, 43 years B. C. [*Qy.* — Did they have cradles in ancient Salmo ?] Next, making a leap over time and space, see Robert Bruce, a dear, sonsie little bud of a king, shaking his tiny Scotch fist at England in the March of 1274 ; next in 1516 see Conrad Gesner at Zurich on the 26th, a few hours old, unconscious that he is destined to be one of the noblest men, one of the most learned philosophers, of his day; and, all the while, Botany is waiting for him to grow up and introduce her to the world as a science. And then, in March, 1596, take a peep at the helpless, new-born Descartes, whose philosophies shall one day muddle mankind.

Step onward, please, into the eighteenth century, — March 29, 1738.

Who is this little creature, with his soft, peachy cheek, and his smiling mouth, already a miniature copy of his beautiful French mother? Be careful! It is Joseph Guillotin: already he may have taken a hint from the carven cradle-top over his head. That same Joseph, in his humanity, not his cruelty, shall one day tell the National Assembly to put its victims to death, if they must do it at all, with mercy and skill; and he will make them a guillotine for the purpose.

While Joseph is still a child, promoted to marbles and kites, and proud of his ten years of boyhood, we can visit another March cradle (23, 1749), containing Peter Simon Laplace, swaddled in flannel, but smiling a meaning baby-smile. Who knows? Perhaps spirit voices are telling him of all that he shall live to accomplish. No: the smile is too simple for that. I think it is because he hears that Napoleon will some day make him a count, that Louis XVIII. will honor him still further. Moving onward, we note a grave also. Its stone is dated March 5, 1827; and beneath it sleeps the form of the Marquis de Laplace.

Ah! here is a cradle, all trimmed with snowy muslin and ribbons! It is only a girl-baby, to be sure, and the parents are plain people; and there is a shock-headed boy of twelve peeping in at the door, asking when he can

kiss his new sister.   But see what the father, a well-known
musician of his day, is writing on a certain leaf of the family Bible !   It is German ; but we can translate it : "Born
March 16, 1750, Caroline Lucretia Herschel."   The boy
William, standing outside, will be proud of his sister one
of these days.

Two years later, on the 16th, another little girl, destined
to be famous, opened her eyes to the light.   She is remembered now as Madame Campan, the French histori-
cal writer.

There are not, I believe, many more March cradles
worth noting.   That of the renowned Dr. Chalmers grew
heavier, by a baby's weight, on the 17th of March, 1780 ;
and so, precisely one year afterward, did that of Ebenezer
Elliott, the Corn Law Rhymer.

Still another cradle was filled, on the 18th, in 1782.
Fortunately the rockers, not believing in independent
sovereignty, moved in unison, or the little John C. Cal-
houn would not have slept so peacefully.   Sixty-eight
years afterward, a March grave opened to receive the
weary body of the South Carolina statesman.

Re-crossing the ocean, we wander into a darkened room
over a butcher's shop, in the town of Nottingham, England.   There is a baby here (March 21, 1787), who will
one day be a butcher-boy, next a stocking-weaver, then a
lawyer's clerk, then a dying student of divinity at Cam-
bridge ; through all displaying qualities of heart and mind
that have rendered the name of Henry Kirke White honored beyond his generation.   Only twenty-one years on
earth ; but what a lesson he gave of patient perseverance,
of indomitable energy, of lofty will, that even the tyranny
of bodily infirmity could not subdue !

There is yet another March cradle, — a cradle so suggestive, so fraught with deep philosophies and reflections,
that one almost rebels at skipping past it in a paragraph.
But there is no alternative. Let us be content to see that
it is a beautiful cradle, furnished with imperial magnifi-
cence ; that the very air floating about it is perfumed with
the breath of a palace ; that the hopes and prayers of a
nation cluster around its downy pillows. And, after all,
it holds only an ordinary infant. Ah ! If Josephine had
been the mother, all might have ended so differently !
But I must not moralize nor speculate. The wisest plan
is to call in Capt. Cuttle. Overhaul your French history,
March 20, 1811, and, when found, stick a pin in it.

It is not pleasant to hunt up old graves as it is to
peer into cradles, because, even with faith pointing up-
wards, our thoughts *will* crawl under the slabs and monuments in search of our so-called dead. To the freed souls
looking on, how strange this must seem !

Still visible among the débris of ages, are the sculp-
tured names of Phocion, the great Athenian, as good as
he was great, who died in March, 317 years B. C. ; and
Cæsar and Mark Antony, and many other famous men of
antiquity, who, according to the best authorities, closed
their earthly career in the waking month.

All along the highways of history we can find March
graves, and in the narrower and more winding paths of
life we see them proudly rearing their inscriptions to the
daylight. Our time is short : we must read them as we
run.

Among those of the seventeenth century, we meet with
the name of a player distinguished in his art, immortal

20*

from the fact that his fellow-actor Shakspeare saw him play Hamlet and Romeo and Macbeth, — one Burbage, who made his final "exit" on the 16th of March, 1619. Also we find in 1640 Philip Massinger, whose life, though illumed by bright gifts, was but one long winter's day; and Charlotte Tremouille (1663), a shining star among heroic women; and, in 1677, Wenceslaus Hollar, the famous but luckless engraver of Bohemia, whose works, it is said, numbered nearly twenty-four hundred plates.

In the eighteenth century we find honored names. Here is Sebastian de Vauban, the greatest military engineer of France (March 30, 1707); next, Sir Isaac Newton, who, winding his watch on the 20th of March, 1727, fell back, and spoke no more; next, Jean Baptist Rousseau, the celebrated French poet, who died in banishment on the 17th, 1741; Laurence Sterne, a non-reverend divine, who, nevertheless, had veins of pure gold in his earthy nature (18th, 1766); William Smith, the English geologist, (23d, 1769); Swedenborg, father of one faith, and thought-giver to many another (29th, 1772); and, last of all, one of England's polished ornaments, Lord Chesterfield, who on March 24, 1773, after Dayroles was comfortably seated, closed his eyes, and died, as he had lived, a gentleman.

Now we come to fresher graves, though scarcely greener memories. Only a few of the names can be read in such a hasty glance as this, — among them John Horne Tooke (March 18, 1812), renowned in English politics, and none the worse for a word-combat with that writer in an iron mask, the immortal Junius; and, greater than all, the name of Goethe, whose dying request for "more light" was gloriously answered on March 22, 1832.

There are others, whose monuments are plainly visible ; but, as their names have already been mentioned, we view them silently, and pass on.

Here are two, on opposite sides of the British Channel, but bearing the same date, March 21, 1843. One tells of Baron La Motte Fouqué, dear to the hearts of France ; the other, of Robert Southey, poet-laureate of England.

Twice since then, — in 1855 and 1860, — has March, with bated breath, whispered the summons to those whom the world would fain have kept a little longer, — Anna Jameson and Charlotte Brontë. They have grown so dear to us, these two, that we will not call them dead. The homes of the immortals may be nearer than we think.

And now, is not March a memorable month ? Ask Nature ; ask the busy, ever-changing world ; ask the Christian Church, constant in her memories ; ask March herself. If any one can blow her own trumpet, surely it is she.

The Rights of the Body.

———◆———

RUCIFY the flesh, if you will : that's all well enough in its way; but honor the flesh too, say I. Second in importance only to the human soul, the body cannot in itself be low and base. In many ways the body shapes and colors the soul, even as the soul colors and shapes the body. Therefore I repeat, honor it, study it. It has to hold *you* while you are here : therefore hold you it reverently and with care so long as you are in it.

The jests and gibes that are flung at the human body! The absurd conjectures and insinuations! The contemptble comparisons!

"What of its vaunted powers?" sneers one. "Can it build like a bee, scent like a hound, sleep like a toad, hold on like a leech, jump like a grasshopper, or climb like a monkey?" "And its voice!" says another. "Why, if the volume of a human voice bore the relative proportion to a man's size that the note of a canary bears to the bird's exquisite form, his lightest word could be heard at a distance of eight hundred miles." And still another malcontent has suggested, that "if man only had,

236

relatively to his bulk, the jumping power of the tiniest flea, he could spring from New York to China at a single bound!"

"If he had proportionately the jumping powers of a flea," forsooth! Stuff and nonsense! The idea of a rational being jumping from New York to China! A man never was intended to be like a flea. If you put your finger on him, is he not there?—unless he owes you money, which, of course, alters the case.

It is one of the growing evils of the age,—this speaking so lightly of the noble human creature. I cannot express the indignation with which I read yesterday the following precious item, by a scientific writer:—

"If a man, weighing one hundred and forty pounds, were squeezed in a hydraulic press, seventy pounds of water would run out, the balance being solid matter. A man is, chemically speaking, forty-five pounds of carbon and other elements, with nitrogen, diffused through five and a half pailfuls of water."

Think of that! There's a pretty bit of information to introduce into the sanctity of home; to pour into the ears of growing boys and girls! Where would Mr. Snapp's dignity be, I'd like to know, if the children understood that he was only "half and half," like his sometime beverage? What if, after he had delivered a few impressive words of paternal rebuke and counsel to the children, I should say to them, "Don't mind your father, my dears: he's only a little carbon, nitrogen, and other elements, diffused through five and a half pailfuls of water"? A pretty state of things we should have after that!

No, my friends: joking aside, this sort of thing will not

do. You must respect the body, and teach your children to do likewise. It's the best material thing that Heaven has made yet; and I don't believe it's going to be excelled in this world.

Far be it from me to suppress the truth. If it can be scientifically demonstrated that our most solid men are really five and a half pailfuls of water, let the fact stand: that is a mere question of condition. What I beg leave to uphold is the dignity of the human body as we know it, and not under the hydraulic press. Therefore again I say, respect the body, dear men and women. Speak of it reverently, as it deserves. Behold, how fine a thing it is I "in form and moving how express and admirable!"

Respect the body: study its needs, and meet them. Don't take it into unworthy places; give it sunshine, pure air, and exercise. Be conscientious as to what you put down its throat. Remember, what is fun to the cook and confectioner may be death to *it*. Treat it at least as well as you would your pet horse or hound. Give it good, wholesome food; let it be on intimate terms with friction and soap and water; and especially don't render it ridiculous by your way of dressing it.

Recognize the dignity of the body: hold it erect when you're awake, and let it lie out straight when you're asleep. Don't let it go through the world with little mincing steps, nor great gawky strides. Don't swing its arms overmuch, and don't let them grow limp from inactivity. Resolve to respect its shoulders, its back, its fair proportions generally; and straightway shall struts and stoops and wriggles be unknown forever.

Respect the body: give it what it requires, and no

more. Don't pierce its ears, strain its eyes, or pinch its feet; don't roast it by a hot fire all day, and smother it under heavy bed-covering all night; don't put it in a cold draught on slight occasions, and don't nurse or pet it to death: don't dose it with doctor's stuffs ; and, above all, don't turn it into a wine-cask or a chimney. Let it be " warranted not to smoke " from the time your manhood takes possession.

Respect the body: don't over-work, over-rest, nor over-love it, and never debase it ; but be able to lay it down when you are done with it, a well-worn but not a misused thing. Through all your days, let it walk hand in hand with your noblest self ; and, my word for it, though it will not jump to China at a bound, you'll find it a most excellent thing to have — especially in the country.

Woman's Driving.

'M out of breath; for I've just been off driving with our neighbor, Mrs. G——, who held the reins, and frightened me nearly to death. But, out of breath or not, I must speak my mind before I take off my bonnet. As for Mrs. G——, I have nothing to say of her. She's a good neighbor on foot; and, if she had chanced to be the only survivor of any one of the ten accidents that miraculously didn't happen this morning, my heart tells me she would have mourned me truly, and comforted poor John as well as she could. But this I will say: no woman ought to attempt to drive a horse, until she knows precisely how to harness and unharness that noble animal; no woman should drive, who cannot distinguish "a shy" from symptoms of blind staggers; no woman should drive, who hasn't presence of mind, who hasn't a firm hand, who can't fasten a tie-strap, or who gasps out, "Whoa-a-a, sir!" to a frightened horse, as if she were about to faint. Neither should a woman drive, who at one moment lets the reins go flippetty-flap on the horse's back, jerks them violently the next; or who, unskilled in peremptory coaxing or the use of the lash, is constantly inflicting feeble horizontal whippings with the entire length of the lines. And, more than all, a woman who believes that only slow horses are safe should never be trusted with any human life but her own. These wretched pokes of horses, that stumble and back and stop just when they ought not, that are too sleepy to heed the lines, and too stupid to be turned around in a space not big enough for a camel-dance, are the special pets of poor drivers among our gentle sex ; yet how very dangerous such horses are !

I know what I am saying. Some women can drive, and some can not ; and those who *can* will not consider the above remarks at all personal. They feel their power, and take a pride in the art. They know how every failure a woman makes in any department hurts the credit of every other woman who ever afterward may express a desire to attempt to do any thing. A man may meet twenty poor male drivers in an hour, and his comment, if he has noticed their deficiencies at all, will be that they were " not half men," they didn't know how to drive ; but, if they see one female driver who fails to handle the reins skilfully, they straightway decide, and declare for years to come, that a woman can't drive, and that's the long and short of it.

So, dear sisters, be considerate. For the credit of all womankind, know what you are about when you attempt the slightest feat of horsemanship. Put your judgment into the work ; learn the practical bearings of the undertaking. They're simple enough. Take up common-sense with your reins, and resolution with your whip ; and never for a moment allow a mere animal to make you forget

21

your human superiority.   Telegraph your soul through
the lines, if you can ; be brave, brisk, calm, and mag-
netic, or don't ask me to go out with you in your lovely
new buggy.

There, I feel better !   I'll ask Mrs. G—— over to
tea.

United Ages.

 MAY not be a Bedlam maniac, as Susan Nipper would say, but there are some things in this world that do make me right up and down mad ! One of these is the ridiculous way certain newspaper folk and domestic wonder-mongers have of announcing the united ages of a number of persons by way of producing — uncommon sense only knows what.

Certainly not astonishment, for early in life we cease to start at the proposition that eighty and seventy make a hundred and fifty ; surely not a sense of the sublime, since the idea of a dozen ordinary persons being able to constitute one Methuselah almost robs the great patriarchal fact of its grandeur ; and most decidedly not amusement, for the thought of thus Siamesing so many infirm human existences is dismal to the extreme.

What, then, can induce any one to unite ages ? or is it I who am at fault, being too dull to perceive the majesty of a conglomerate individual ?

No : if three or more aged men happen to be together, they are three aged men, and that's all there is about it. You can't make a triple-headed veteran out of the lot, any more than you can make a forty-pound fish out of a shoal of minnows. As for trying to make a human addition sum out of the three, it is enough to make Old Time throw his hour-glass at the head of the calculator.

Only yesterday I read in a morning paper, an account of an interesting family reunion on the event of a fine old gentleman reaching the ripe age of ninety-three. So far, so good. It was a beautiful occasion to celebrate. There were the descendants, plenty of them, and all in regular order. Still no offence. Nobody could expect an old gentleman of ninety-three to have a grand family reunion without any descendants. The account put me in quite a glow of kindly feeling, when suddenly, without the least warning, I came upon this exhausting paragraph : —

" The combined ages of the children, grandchildren, and great-grandchildren are seven hundred and sixteen years."

Think of that, now! that is, if you *can* think of it. I can't. I tried at first to divide the whole into children, grandchildren, and great-grandchildren ; and they spread out indefinitely from a dozen to a hundred. Then, scanning the account further, I managed to discover that there were four children, eighteen grandchildren, and seven great-grandchildren. Ah! thought I, now we have it! The combined number of these is 29 ; and 29 goes into 716 — goes into 716 — about twenty-four or twenty-five times. What then? Should I, by making each of the combined nearly twenty-five years old, rob the grandfathers and grandmothers of two-thirds of their natural lives, and make the baby great-grandchildren exceedingly backward for their age? or should I calculate the thing on a common-sense basis, and allow a difference of about twenty years to each generation? Absurd! I scorned to do either. It's a case for the lightning-calculator in his dotage!

Again, we sometimes hear of a pew-full of elderly citizens whose united ages, we are told, amount to, say four hundred years. What of it? What good does it do? Are we to understand that there were six hoary individuals in the pew, each of them crowned with sixty-six years and eight months? Probably not. Were there three, each of them about a hundred and thirty-three last Christmas? Preposterous! Then perhaps there were four, and each of them —

" But," interposes your startling announcer, "the number is known. There were five." Ah! that simplifies matters at once. Undoubtedly they were just eighty years old apiece; or, if not, they ought to have been, or else seated themselves in separate pews, and not disturbed the meeting by suggesting arithmetical conundrums.

This sort of thing, I repeat, makes me furious. If it is done at all, it should be done thoroughly, and on a grand scale. Let the morning papers, for instance, come out with something like this : —

" Broadway presented a remarkable spectacle yesterday afternoon, — remarkable even for this most wonder-presenting thoroughfare of our metropolis. The streets were thronged with our oldest and most respectable citizens, many of whom carried gold-headed canes. United ages of all pedestrians between Fourteenth and Vesey Streets, at the time our reporter left, 8,673,043,271,975 years."

Or, perhaps, this : —

21*

"BY TELEGRAPH — ANOTHER TERRIBLE DISASTER. — We shudder to record that the Pacific Railroad express-train to San Francisco, in consequence of a misprint in the time-table, last evening collided with a freight train in a gorge of the Rocky Mountains. The train was loaded to excess. Nobody killed; but every passenger was paralyzed for over ten minutes by the shock. Tender infants, blooming maidens, middle-aged parents, and venerable grandsires — one and all shared the same fate. Some idea of the extent of this dreadful calamity may be gathered from the fact that the aggregated ages of the passengers amount to 52,089,742,301½ years!"

Horrible! Figuring this out carefully, by *def*erential calculus, it would make our very venerable monster of an Aggregate motionless and helpless for six years, five months, four days, and twenty minutes. Once let an idea like that be impressed upon the public mind, and railroad companies will have to look out!

Or, for a change, let somebody publish the fact, that in a certain ward of the Scroogstown Foundling Asylum, there are fifty individuals whose united ages make just two years! This would be vastly more interesting, and wouldn't tax one's arithmetic so cruelly.

And now, my friends, as our dear old parson used to say (and he was a responsible man, I'm sure, because his "united ages," taking in wife and eight children, amounted to at least three hundred and ninety-two years), we'll conclude.

Hold! A thought staggers me! Purchasers of this volume, probably sixty thousand; readers, at least three hundred thousand; combined ages of these, not in years, but in minutes, would be —

The thought is too immense ! Let them wait until S. S. is no more. Then let the sum total of the years of all her readers be calculated for the benefit of inquiring friends ; but let it never be inscribed upon the monumental stone erected by sorrowing kindred over

ONE

WHO DID NOT BELIEVE

IN

STUFF AND NONSENSE.